ATTACK OF THE VINEH

There were at least twenty of them, clawing their way out of an overgrown ravine and coming straight for us. Keeshah roared his challenge, leaped forward, slashing and snapping at the nearest vineh. Then Tarani and I were left behind, rolling on the ground.

A vineh thudded down on top of me. A hairy arm grabbed me around the throat and jerked, nearly twisting my head off. The pain and lack of air canceled out my eyesight, and I saw the swirling, undefined colors of unconsciousness closing in on me . . .

The pressure was released suddenly and I could breathe. When my vision cleared, I saw Tarani pulling her sword out of a vineh's back . . .

THE BRONZE OF EDDARTA

Third Volume in the Gandalara Cycle
by Randall Garrett and Vicki Ann Heydron

THE GANDALARA CYCLE

III
THE BRONZE OF EDDARTA

RANDALL GARRETT and **VICKI ANN HEYDRON**

BANTAM BOOKS
TORONTO · NEW YORK · LONDON · SYDNEY

THE BRONZE OF EDDARTA
A Bantam Book / May 1983

Map by Robert J. Sabuda.

ISBN 0-553-23281-9

Published simultaneously in the United States and Canada

Bantam Books are published by Bantam Books, Inc. Its trademark, consisting of the words ''Bantam Books'' and the por-
trayal of a rooster, is Registered in U.S. Patent and Trademark
Office and in other countries. Marca Registrada. Bantam
Books, Inc., 666 Fifth Avenue, New York, New York 10103.

PRINTED IN THE UNITED STATES OF AMERICA

O   0 9 8 7 6 5 4 3 2 1

THE BRONZE OF EDDARTA

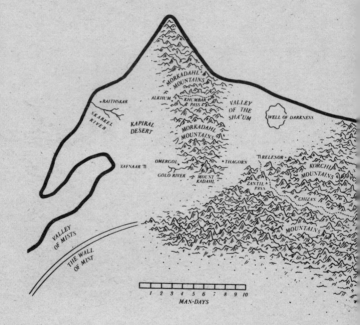

RAITHSKAR

SKARKEL RIVER

KAPIRAL DESERT

MORKADAHL MOUNTAINS

ALKIHUM

KHUMBAR PASS

VALLEY OF THE SHA'UM

WELL OF DARKNESS

MORKADAHL MOUNTAINS

YAFNAAR TI

OMERGOL

THAGORN

RELENOR

KORCHIA MOUNTAINS

GOLO RIVER

MOUNT KADAHL

ZANTIL PASS

CHIZAN

MOUNTAINS

VALLEY OF MISTS

THE WALL OF MIST

1 2 3 4 5 6 7 8 9 10
MAN-DAYS

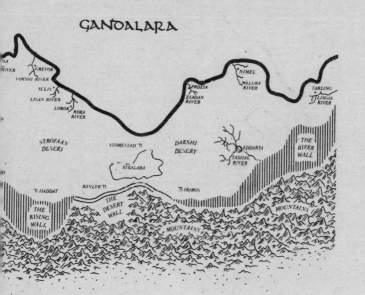

PRELIMINARY PROCEEDINGS:
INPUT SESSION THREE

—Ah, it is you. Is it time to begin once more?

—If it suits you, Recorder.

—And your shoulder?

—The pain of the remembered wound has faded, as you said it would. I feel quite well again, and ready to continue.

—Then be comfortable, and we will prepare by reviewing the material you have already given to the All-Mind.

You spoke of the uniting of two lives, one nearly ended, one barely begun. You were Ricardo Carillo, in a world outside the Walls of Gandalara. You saw a fireball, which you call a meteor, and after an undetermined period of unconsciousness, you awoke in Gandalara, sharing the body—and some of the memories—of a young man named Markasset.

—And sharing his telepathic bond with a member of Gandalara's intelligent feline species, a sha'um.

—Markasset's father, Thanasset, was implicated in the theft of a political treasure, a jewel called the Ra'ira.

—At first, I wanted only to prove that Thanasset—a man I liked and respected as soon as I met him—was innocent. Later, however, I accepted the task of recovering the gem and returning it to its protected place in Raithskar.

—A duty you shouldered reluctantly.

—That's a little unfair, Recorder. I had no idea, at first, that the Ra'ira was anything more than an ordinary, if uncommonly valuable, gemstone. In Ricardo's world, such beautiful jewels had often been surrounded with a mys-

1

tique of charm or danger. I assumed that the Ra'ira had attracted a connection with the transfer of political power.

—I meant no implication of blame. I Record; I do not judge.

—And I must apologize for my short temper. The fact is, I suppose, that I blame myself. Perhaps if I hadn't spent so much time trying to avoid responsibility for the Ra'ira . . .

—Such speculation is useless to the All-Mind.

—Of course it is. Again, my apologies.

—In any case, when you discovered the true nature of the Ra'ira, you didn't hesitate to commit yourself to its recovery.

—By then, I felt I had no choice. Only a few people knew how dangerous the Ra'ira could be. It was a tele-pathic tool, a transmitter which could amplify the native mind-talent of a Gandalaran. The ancient Kings had used the Ra'ira to keep absolute control over Gandalara.

—You shiver. Are you cold?

—The image of the old Kingdom makes me shudder. Ricardo had some experience with societies in which expressing an opinion that disagreed with governmental precepts could send an individual into confinement, or worse. The concept of watching every word you say is appalling enough, but under the corrupt Kings, your very thoughts could betray disloyalty or discontent. I hadn't quite believed Thanasset when he told me that the slaves, sent as tribute to the last Kings, never rebelled against their lot. Once I understood about the Ra'ira, I could see how fearful they must have been . . . how demoralized . . . how utterly without hope.

—You said you felt you had no choice but to pursue the Ra'ira. Was it because of your sympathy for the ancient slaves?

—Yes, and because somebody had to do it. Thymas and Tarani and I were convinced that we had been brought together for the purpose of opposing Gharlas's insane plan to reconstruct the Kingdom. If he tried, we were sure he would succeed only in creating a civil war that would destroy and demoralize Gandalara. We weren't sure we

2

could stop him—but we knew we had to try to return the Ra'ira to the protective custody of the Council of Supervisors in Raithskar.

—Are you ready to continue the Record?

—I am ready, Recorder.

—Then make your mind one with mine, as I have made mine one with the All-Mind . . .

                o
               o
              o
             o
              o
               o
                o
              o
             o
              o
               o

WE BEGIN!

1

I was on my way back to Volitar's old workshop. I had been to the market area of the city to "mail" some letters and buy a map. Both letters were already on their way to Raithskar—one by caravan, the other tied to the leg of a *maufa*, the fast-flying message bird of Gandalara.

Caravans could move no faster than their *vleks*, the goat-size pack animals that were only slightly more stupid than stubborn. It would take Illia's "Dear Jane" letter nearly fifty days to reach her. It was possible—not likely, but possible—that I could be back in Raithskar with the Ra'ira before she got that letter, and I approved of that idea.

Illia had loved Markasset, and his memory of that relationship made Illia very special to me. I felt I owed it to her to tell her, in person, that I couldn't just settle into the ordinary domestic life she and Markasset might have shared.

It was also possible that I wouldn't get back to Raithskar alive. That's why I had written the letter—it was better than letting her believe that I hadn't thought of her at all after our sweet farewell.

Thanasset would receive his letter in only a few days, the bird-handler had assured me. His maufa wouldn't take it directly to Raithskar, because he couldn't direct a bird to a place where he, himself, had never been. His maufa would take the message to another *maufel* in Chizan, who would send it with one of his own birds.

5

I had watched, fascinated, while the old man had held the small gray-green bird in front of his face. He had laid his forefinger against its white bill, and stared into one bright eye for a few seconds before flinging it up into the air. I watched the bird fly, the thin strip of leather trailing after it, until it was out of sight.

That's another kind of mind skill, I realized. *Like a Recorder's conscious link with the collective memory of the All-Mind. Like a Rider's telepathic bond with his sha'um. Those skills are—well, not common. But accepted, at least.*

It's the "mindpower," the ability to influence another person's mind, that's scary. Tarani has it, and it scares her. Gharlas has it, and HE scares ME. I have some resistance to his power because I'm "double-minded," and it's non-Gandalaran Ricardo who controls Markasset's body and memories. But even I'm not immune to it. The sooner we take Gharlas out of action, the better.

The letter to Thanasset told him, in guarded terms, what I was doing. He was one of the Supervisors, and he knew what the Ra'ira was. He had tried to get me appointed to the Council so that I could be told the truth. My message to him was, essentially: "I understand. I'll bring it back."

When the bird had finally disappeared, I had gone to several letterers, looking for a map that would tell me where Eddarta was. Markasset had only the vaguest notion, which didn't surprise me. His interests had been more physical than scholarly—a trait which had saved "our" life more than once.

I was delighted to find a map which showed *all* of Gandalara, and with that important piece of parchment folded and tucked into my belt, I started the climb back to Tarani and Thymas.

Dyskornis sprawled across the feet of the rising hills which supported three tiers of glassmaking workshops, built out from steep slopes so as to make annual replacement of the breakable firebowls under the glass kilns practical. Further down the hill, a smaller, noisier city catered to the trade of transients. Beyond that lay marked lots planted with the hard-wooded trees that provided glassmakers with heat during one work season, and ash for the glass mix in the next.

Following the road, I walked between open fields with their grasslike ground cover. A writhing shape of tan, bright against the green, caught my eye—Keeshah, rolling in the glossy field.

Come here, and I'll scratch that itch for you, I invited him.

He rolled once more, then stood up from the greenery. He was more than ten yards away from me, but I could see the glint of his tusks as his lips pulled back from a huge yawn. He came toward me slowly, and I left the road to meet him halfway. I was fascinated by the ripple of muscle across his broad chest, which was almost on the same level as my shoulder. When we met, I reached under the massive wedge of his head to scratch his chest first.

Feels good, he told me. He laid his bulk on the ground and rolled half over.

Hey, I thought it was your back that itched, I thought though I put both hands to work, combing torn plants out of the thick, pale fur on the sha'um's belly.

Itch everywhere, he complained. *Don't like this place.*

When we leave, Keeshah, we'll be on the road for a long time. How are your wounds doing?

Following the directions of my hands and mind, he rolled over to his stomach and crouched patiently while I searched through his fur for the remnants of the scratches and gouges he had taken during his fight with the other sha'um. They were no more than faint lines in the newly healed skin.

I was surprised, but in the next instant I reminded myself that Tarani's gift of healing sleep had shortened my own recovery by at least half. I flexed my right shoulder; all that remained of the double stab wound was a twinge, and even that seemed noticeably less sharp than it had yesterday.

A far-off rumbling sound washed down the hillside to us, and Keeshah and I both looked up toward Volitar's workshop. Standing half in, half out of the downslope shade was Thymas's sha'um, Ronar. He looked in our direction for a moment, then paced into the light, paused, turned, and paced back into shadow.

Was that comment directed at us? I asked Keeshah.

No.

His mind closed down around that answer, as it always did when he discussed the other sha'um—or, for that matter, the sha'um's master. I scratched idly where Keeshah liked it the most, just at the base of his neck, while I watched the other cat pacing.

As far as I had learned in Gandalara, the direct mind-to-mind communication which Keeshah and I shared was a unique bond between a sha'um and his Rider. I had talked with Tarani about her link with the huge white bird who had been with her for four years. It was a limited kind of communication, consisting only of images, and requiring intense concentration. It also seemed hard for the maufel to give his instructions to his bird. Keeshah and I maintained a constant, nearly subconscious link. Intense emotions, especially fear or anger, flowed readily along that link. Conversation required a conscious decision, but not much effort.

Among themselves, sha'um used vocal and physical signals, and except for rare people like Tarani and Gharlas, the Gandalarans had to depend on voice and attitude. But Riders had a special . . . well, sometimes it might be considered a handicap. No matter what a man pretended, or really wanted to believe, his true feelings were mirrored in the action of his sha'um.

Tarani had been the one to tell me that. Ronar had refused to allow her to ride him, but Keeshah had accepted her as second rider without hesitation. She had pointed out that their behavior reflected our attitudes, and there was no denying the truth of it.

Thymas, entrenched in the male-militarist traditions of the Sharith, had been scandalized by the idea. Both Markasset and Ricardo had grown up free of Sharith tradition, so Rikardon's decision was based only on consideration of Tarani's comfort. Her alternative to riding one of the sha'um had been swinging and bouncing between the huge cats in a cargo net.

So I tried, now, to read what Ronar could tell me about Thymas. The boy had told me he was impatient to get going, in spite of the fact that he and Ronar were only partially healed. I had been hearing his words as false bravado, but in watching Ronar, I realized that he really was feeling restless and confined.

And what, I wondered, *is Keeshah saying about the way I feel? Am I—*

Bored, came Keeshah's complaint, as if in answer. I laughed. He raised up on his forelegs a little, and swung his head suddenly, catching me in the side and knocking me into an ungainly somersault.

"Hey—mmph!" I yelled. I came upright spitting greenery and skidding down the slope. Before I could get good purchase, I felt a whack on my shoulders, and I was tumbling again. I yelped once more when my injured shoulder caught all my weight. I let my body relax; one last roll, and I slid to a halt, facedown.

I lay there, keeping both mind and body as still as I could. I couldn't hear Keeshah approach, but I could feel his breath on my neck when his anxious thought reached me.

Rikardon?

It was a though time had turned back, and I lay upon salty sand, instead of the fragrant grassy stuff in which my face was buried. Keeshah had called me Markasset then . . .

I had meant to "play dead" as a joke on Keeshah. By the time I realized how cruel that was, I couldn't give up the ruse because I was caught up in a memory, immobilized by it.

It wasn't *my* memory. It was Keeshah's.

I felt the torrent of his anguish as Markasset died, felt in my own throat Keeshah's scream of grief, in my own hands and feet the pull of the killer's flesh against his razor claws. I grieved for the emptiness in his mind. I ached for the touch of hand on fur.

I felt his need to run, to roar, to speak to his own kind, in his own way, of the lost kinship. And I felt the other need, the strange one, the unbidden knowing. The need to *wait*.

I felt his wonder when he sensed new life within the dead shell of his friend. I felt his caution, his hesitation, his awareness that this new person would perish without his help.

In Keeshah's persona, I accepted responsibility for myself.

In Keeshah's memory, I touched the stranger's mind— my own—and found it strong and clear, but needful.

As Keeshah, I accepted Ricardo.

I *was* Keeshah, and every muscle thrilled with the joy of the bond with my new friend, with a fierce pride in our partnership . . .

Suddenly, I was back in the present, nearly overcome by the unexpected sharing of Keeshah's intimate memory, totally ashamed of having frightened him.

I rolled over, and Keeshah snapped his head back in surprise.

Keeshah, I rushed into the apology, *I'm sorry. I'm not really hurt—hey! What the! . . .*

It never crossed my mind to be afraid of Keeshah, even though my own reaction to that sort of joke would have been anger. But I wasn't prepared for his surge of gladness. He was so happy that I wasn't hurt that he forgot I *could* be. A sha'um's idea of mischief . . .

When I dragged myself through the door of the two-story house attached to Volitar's workshop, Thymas and Tarani both stared at me in amazement. I looked down at my clothes. Blue tunic and tan trousers, even my leather boots, carried ground-in green and brown stains. I felt an itch behind my ear, slapped an unbeautiful insectish creature to the floor, and stepped on it.

"Keeshah was bored," I said.

2

I wasn't expecting a roar of laughter, but I had hoped for a smile or two. Tarani tried to oblige, but the shape of humor didn't rest well in her tense face. I glanced at Thymas, sitting sullenly on his pallet, pretending to mend a cargo net that was perfectly whole, and I understood how she felt. She had been alone with Thymas most of the day, and the boy's self-loathing was a tangible, oppressive burden to anyone around him.

"I saw Ronar moving around," I said. "How is he feeling, Thymas?"

"He is nearly healed," the boy said. He threw down the net and stood up with nearly his old grace. If I hadn't been watching for it, I never would have seen the flash of pain in his eyes as he stretched the muscles around the still-mending wound in his side. "We are ready to travel."

Now, everybody in the room knew that was an out-and-out lie. Ronar had lain low for days after his fight with Keeshah, before he came forward to offer my sha'um his undefended throat. That gesture of surrender was partially Thymas's idea—a reflection of the boy's guilt feelings—but it could never have happened if Ronar hadn't been badly injured and demoralized, himself. Tarani had used her hypnotic/psychic skills to help him, but Thymas's sha'um had slept only one night under her spell. The body healed itself faster in that restful sleep, but it still needed a minimum of time to do the job. Ronar was hardly "ready

11

to travel"—at least, not at the grueling pace we had kept since leaving Thagorn.

But I said: "Good. We'll leave in the morning, then."

I walked over to the dining table, unfolding the map which I had, fortunately, lost during Keeshah's first assault, and later retrieved. I ignored Tarani's questioning look, and spread the parchment out on the table.

"The Walls of the World." I had wondered about that term, while I was still only Ricardo. When I had acquired Markasset's memories, I had also, inevitably, acquired his viewpoints. At every opportunity, I made a conscious effort to step aside from them, but lately there hadn't been much opportunity. I'd been worrying too hard about staying alive to think much about Markasset's complacent acceptance of the limits of his world.

Now, in a two-dimensional image of Gandalara, the edges of the "world" were clearly marked.

As in the fragmented maps I *had* seen, a thick, dark line winding its way across one long edge of the map represented the Great Wall. Gandalaran charting conventions placed the Great Wall at the top of the map. Though I was sure the Wall didn't run truly east-west, it did mark the northern edge of Gandalara, so Ricardo was fairly comfortable with using such a map.

The southern border was marked off into sections. At the left edge of the map was a feature with the intriguing name of Valley of Mists. From it, the Wall of Mist ran eastward below the Kapiral Desert toward the Morkadahl Mountains, where it merged into the unnamed mountain range which butted up against the Korchis to form the Chizan Passage. East of the Zantro Pass, one of the two high crossings that enclosed Chizan, the southern wall was divided into three sections. The Rising Wall began at Inid, the Refreshment House at the foot of the slope leading down from the Zantro. It approached a plateau isolated from the walls, and became the Desert Wall. Further east, it was known as the River Wall.

I put the index finger of my right hand on a spot marked in the middle of the River Wall. "This is Eddarta," I explained to Thymas and Tarani, who were looking over my shoulders. I hooked a chair out with my foot, and sat down to give them a clearer view.

"And Dyskornis is here." Tarani touched the map.

Thymas studied the area between our markings. "Gharlas will take the quickest route," he said. "Tarani—which way?"

Without hesitation, Tarani said: "South." She moved her finger as she talked. "The main caravan route to Eddarta follows the line of Refreshment Houses. Inid. Haddat. Kanlyr. Iribos. You have said that Gharlas was a caravan master—that is the way he must have traveled before."

The shortest way home is the way you know best, I thought. *She's probably right.*

Thymas was peering at the map closely, muttering to himself. "Five days to Inid, another five to Haddat. He's four days ahead, but with the sha'um..." He tilted his head. "We should catch up with him midway between Haddat and Kanlyr."

"Correction," I said. "We *would* catch up with him—*if* he went that way, which I think is likely, and *if* we followed him, which we aren't going to do."

"Not follow—"

I held up a hand to cut off Thymas's explosion. "Use your head. There's nothing in that direction but Refreshment Houses. Tarani, you tell us—what is the southern route like?"

"The way from Inid to Kanlyr lies in a trench between dry hills. I have gone no further, but that far, at least, it is a miserable trip." She smiled a little wistfully. "That's why my troupe did so well through there; the caravans were desperate for some distraction from the journey."

I nodded, thinking that Gharlas had traveled the main caravan route regularly between Eddarta and Raithskar, yet had never seen Tarani, who had entertained caravans with her dancing and illusions. The odds against his missing her had to be enormous.

But there's no doubting it—he was astonished when he

finally put it together that Volitar's phantom "niece" was the illusionist he had heard so much about.

Call it destiny, I thought. *Call it fate. Call it scrambled eggs, if you like. But Gharlas wasn't meant to know about Tarani until we all met here in Dyskornis.*

"Right," I said. "So we're going to follow the Great Wall—" I traced the northern route with my finger. "—past all these little towns.

"The reasons we are going to do it this way," I said, forestalling something else Thymas started to say, "are threefold.

"First, there are towns and rivers north of us, which means that the countryside is more hospitable, and it's likely the sha'um can hunt for their meals along the way.

"Second, Gharlas is crazy, but not foolish. He'll expect us to follow him. There's no telling what sort of traps he'll leave along the way.

"Third, I hope he *won't* expect us to be waiting for him in Eddarta when he gets there."

"You mean you're going to let him reach his home territory?" Thymas demanded.

I sighed. *Why is it that the only time he sounds like himself, is when he's arguing with me?*

It was Tarani who answered the boy. "You're forgetting that Gharlas is more than just an Eddartan, Thymas. He's a caravan master. He probably knows every vlek-handler from here to Eddarta. If they do not already owe him service, he can buy them. And those he cannot buy, he can . . . command."

I glanced at Thymas, but he wouldn't meet my eyes.

He's remembering that he nearly killed me, while Gharlas controlled him.

"We're already in his home territory," Tarani continued, in the vibrant voice that contained its own kind of command. She sat down and leaned over the map. "I agree with Rikardon's plan, but that has little weight." She placed her hands flat on the map and lifted her head to look directly at the pale-haired boy. "It does not matter

14

that you *disagree*, Thymas. We will *both* do whatever Rikardon suggests."

Uh-oh.

I waited for the explosion, but it never came—at least, not from Thymas. He squared his shoulders, stared at his boots, and said: "Yes, I see what you mean. I've done enough damage."

I slammed my hand on the table—Tarani snatched her fingers out of the way just in time—and stood up.

"I've had all I can take of your simpering self-importance, Thymas."

Thymas gasped. "But I—"

"You *think* you keep apologizing, but you know what you're really doing? You're trying to take credit, all by yourself, for letting Gharlas get away. *Your* mistakes were the serious ones. *Your* mistakes were the avoidable ones. If *you* had done things right . . .

"You want to talk about stupid mistakes? What idiot, who knew there was a price on his head, went into the rogueworld and flashed Serkajon's sword, so that every thief and assassin in Dyskornis knew who he was?" I stabbed my thumb at my chest. "This one, that's who. *You* didn't let Gharlas get away, Thymas. *We* did. Even Tarani. She could have sent Lonna after Gharlas, but instead she chose to send the bird to help me. If the only important thing is to stop Gharlas, she made the wrong choice.

"She did succeed in saving my life. Maybe you think that *was* the wrong choice!"

"Rikardon!" Tarani's shout cut me off in mid-harangue. I was leaning across the corner of the table, forcing Thymas to back away from me. I straightened up.

"You once told me," she said more gently, "that it is easy for you to say insincere things."

Ouch, I thought. *Touché.*

Thymas tried to read the silent message that passed from Tarani to me, and he was beginning to look angry.

Is that what I'm trying to do? I asked myself. *Provoke him into being as nasty as he used to be? God forbid.*

"Sorry," I said. I rubbed my hand over the short, dark

blond fur on my head, searching for the right words—and sending a small shower of dirt onto the map. "I'm only trying to say that we're a team, and that none of us can take credit or blame alone, from here on out.

"Tarani is right about this—a team needs a leader. For reasons that mystify me, I'm it.

"You're right about something else—there is *nothing* more important than getting the Ra'ira away from Gharlas.

"Trust is the key to teamwork, Thymas. You and Tarani have to trust me to give the right orders, and I have to trust you to follow them. Not because you promised your father to obey me."

Which is yet to happen, I thought. *Wups, "Captain"— could be you need some lessons in trust, yourself.*

"Especially not because," I continued, "you feel you've proved yourself unworthy of command." He flinched a little at that, and I knew I had touched a nerve. "We can't afford your self-pity.

"I'm the first to admit that you and I aren't the best of friends, Thymas, but we *have* fought the same enemy. And we've ridden together."

A muscle along Thymas's jaw tensed and relaxed.

This "boy" is going to be the next Lieutenant of the Sharith, I thought. *He takes that duty very seriously. It's time I showed him that I take HIM seriously.*

"Tarani's power and your sword, Thymas. If I'd had a choice, I couldn't have selected two stronger weapons to use against Gharlas. But an unwilling weapon is more hazard than help. Convince me that I'll have your cooperation—not obedience, mind you, but *cooperation*—or stay behind."

I stopped, wondering if I'd said enough, or too much. The boy was thinking about it; that was a good sign. He leaned heavily on the back of the chair in front of him, looking at me, considering. When he spoke, the meek, whining tone was absent from his voice for the first time since the fight with Gharlas. If I'd done nothing else, I'd taken his mind off his guilt.

"'Trust.' 'Cooperation.' 'Sincerity.'" He quoted the words

16

skeptically. "Here's some sincerity, Rikardon. I don't like you. I don't trust you. And I *still* don't understand why Dharak made you Captain."

Your resentment is showing, Thymas, I thought, but this isn't like your usual fit of temper. Is it possible—barely possible—that we're finally beginning to communicate with one another?

"Dharak was worried that you were going to lead the young Riders after Gharlas," I said. "He thought that if he made me Captain, and *I* told them to stay put, they'd listen. He does believe that I'm *supposed* to be the Captain. But what he really wanted was to avoid the split-up of the Sharith." I let that sink in, then I said: "Dharak still leads the Riders. So will you, when your time arrives."

Thymas was quite for a moment. "Convince *me* of something," he said at last. "Convince me that you're the one who is supposed to lead this 'team.' And while you're at it, tell me what the filth you've been hiding all this time. Show me the same kind of trust you say you want from me."

I heard Tarani's intake of breath, but I didn't give her a chance to say anything.

"That's fair, Thymas, and I wish I could give you clear, objective reasons for it. I can't. It's just something I feel. There is something which I *have* been concealing—not for lack of trust, but because I didn't think your knowing it would be useful to either one of us. I'm a... Visitor. Markasset was killed by one of Gharlas's accomplices. I arrived a few hours later."

I saw a look of revelation cross Thymas's face, and I was sure that I was about to be accused, once more, of being a reincarnation of Serkajon. Because Markasset was descended from the man who had destroyed the corrupt Kingdom, and because I had been given his unique steel sword, that seemed to be the standard conclusion people jumped to when they found out I was a Gandalaran personality returned from the All-Mind.

Of course, that's not what I was, but I had let the few

who knew about me believe it, because the concept was acceptable to them. No one in Gandalara knew the truth about where this "Visitor" had come from.

Ricardo had been cruising the Mediterranean Ocean—a concept in itself unacceptable to the desert-familiar Gandalarans—in the company of the lovely young Antonia Alderuccio when the fireball had somehow transported Ricardo to the Kapiral Desert, Markasset, and Keeshah. That star-covered night, and Antonia, were secret memories that came often to my dreams.

It turned out that I was wrong about what Thymas was thinking.

"That's why Gharlas called you 'double-minded!' " he cried. "Is that why you could break—? . . . Oh."

I didn't say anything while he mulled it over, all his thoughts turned inward. When his eyes refocused, he said: "All right. You've convinced me. Now, what proof will you accept that I'll follow orders?"

"All I need is your word, Thymas, freely given."

3

I was on the slope below the workshop, walking back from the bath-house, when the sudden Gandalaran night overtook me. Although no starlight could penetrate the cloud cover, the diffused moonlight gave a ghostly glow to the large features around me—the road, the fields, the outlines of the workshops. A brighter patch of light marked the upstairs window of Volitar's old living quarters, and I aimed my steps in that direction.

As I neared the downhill entrance of the house, I heard the sound of Tarani's humming, and I was able to separate her from the other dark shapes. Ronar was stretched out on the ground, lying on his side. Tarani was kneeling behind him, touching the ugly, infected gash on the back of his neck with one hand. Her other hand was stroking his head slowly, smoothing the fur between his tapered ears.

While I stood there watching, the cat's labored breathing slowed and softened; his limbs moved slightly as the muscles relaxed into Tarani's hypnotic sleep.

I could resist or accept Tarani's powers. This one I had accepted, benefited from, and enjoyed. It had become harder to resist, and right then I had to shake my head to keep from falling under the spell of her rich, compelling voice.

When Tarani had finished, she stood up and came over to me. She touched my arm and led me away from the house so our voices wouldn't disturb the sleeping cat.

"It would be hypocritical of me, now," she said, "to question your decision, Rikardon. But I am concerned for Ronar and Thymas. You must know that they really aren't ready to travel."

"Tell me something," I said. "Was it easier to put Thymas and Ronar to sleep tonight?"

"Yes," she answered, after thinking about it for a minute. "Yes, it was."

"Staying here was tearing Thymas apart inside, Tarani. He wanted us to get going, but didn't want to be left behind. His sense of duty was in conflict with his desires. And that was another source of guilt for him.

"Sitting still is hard for a man like Thymas. That inner turmoil had to be interfering with your healing. Now that he knows we're all going to *do* something—and now that he and I know where we stand—I'm hoping he'll mend faster."

She laughed and shook her head as she took two quick steps forward. The window's light cast a golden sheen on her fine-boned, pale face as she turned toward me.

"Why is it, Rikardon," she said, "that I have the mindgift, yet you read people more clearly than I?"

She was not speaking of telepathy. She meant what Ricardo would call intuition, or empathy, and what Markasset would define as a strong link with the All-Mind: an ability to compare an individual's actions and attitudes to a wide spectrum of experiences, and to define his motivation.

If Markasset had such a link, it was entirely subconscious in Rikardon. But Ricardo hadn't lived for sixty years without learning something about people. Gandalarans weren't human, physically—their body and facial construction differed slightly from *Homo sapiens*—but their mental and emotional patterns were very human.

"Perhaps it's because I'm older, Tarani."

"You're referring to your . . . other lifetime?"

"Yes."

"What was it like?"

I shrugged. "Ordinary." I felt the usual twinge at the

deception; I let her assume that we shared the same heritage. "I was something of a scholar, something of a fighter."

I was grateful that she didn't pursue her curiosity. She merely nodded. "I expect it was the second one that lets you see what Thymas is feeling."

"I . . . can appreciate something else he feels," I said. *What the hell am I doing?* I asked myself.

"The sha'um," I stammered lamely, and too late.

"Don't back away from it, Rikardon," she said quietly. "You and I—we need to 'know where we stand', too."

She was right, of course. And in the lamplight—in any light—she was beautiful. Even Ricardo would have appreciated Tarani's slim, dancer's body, the high-cheekboned face. She shared the patrician looks of the Lords of Eddarta, which were closer to human facial features. The wide tusks that took the place of canine teeth were there, still, but the supraorbital ridge was less pronounced, the face more narrow. Her unusual dark head fur and the glow of power in her eyes set off her striking appearance—even now, with refracted candlelight wavering across her face.

"Before I walked into Thymas's life, he had everything, Tarani. The respect of the Riders, a guarantee of the future he had aimed for all his life, a woman he hoped to marry. I'm not responsible for the upheaval he has lived through in these past weeks, but I am associated with it.

"He and I made a start, this afternoon, toward—well, not friendship. Call it noncompetition. If I were to . . . say certain things to you right now, that balance would be destroyed."

Her back stiffened. "You seem to know so well what Thymas feels," she said. "Assuming that I am no more than a prize for a footrace, does he think he can still compete for me?"

"You know I didn't mean it that way. Thymas has an abundance of pride. I think he's accepted the fact that the woman he loved was only one dimension of the complex Tarani he's getting to know now. But he knows—more importantly, you and I know—that, within the limits of the personality you showed him, you really did love Thymas.

"Maybe you still do."

"Yes," she admitted, and her stiff posture relaxed. "At least, I still care for him insofar that I would not wish him any further hurt. I do see your point. It is one thing that I have turned away from him. It would be quite another if I turned to you. It would disturb him and disrupt the healing process."

"And we need Thymas healthy when we meet Gharlas," I agreed.

She shook her head. "Your concern goes deeper than that," she said. "I can read that much, at least. In spite of all the trouble he has been to you, in your own way, you care for Thymas, too."

"I said we have ridden together. You know Thymas, and the Sharith."

"A bond of loyalty," she said. Abruptly, she took a couple of paces, then came back.

"I confess that I feel drawn to you, Rikardon. It may be no more than curiosity. It may be a kinship created by what we are trying to do. It may be gratitude for your compassion toward Thymas, and Volitar. Whatever is causing it, the attraction is there, and it is better that we recognize and control it.

"I think you and I must 'stand' apart, for now."

She walked away, leaving me feeling uncertain as to whether something had been settled . . . or begun.

The next morning, Tarani and I walked downhill to the market area of the city, and bought the few supplies we thought we would need. We were still Molik's guests, though the coins Tarani had grabbed out of his lockbox after Thymas had killed the roguelord were dwindling fast. I had been wishing that we could buy some extra clothes to take along, but it looked as though we couldn't quite afford it.

Tarani was holding the parcels which contained bread and dried meat. When she saw me counting, she said: "You are welcome to use Volitar's money."

I pulled the drawstrings of the pouch and tucked it into my belt. Then I picked up my parcels—fruit and the roast fowl we would eat on the first night—and led her away from the market stall.

"Thank you, Tarani," I said, "but I don't think that's wise. Why didn't your uncle—"

"My *father*," she corrected me, with sudden sharpness.

"Why didn't Volitar spend them?" I asked, after a second or two. "You said yourself, he never lived more than comfortably."

"They are Eddartan coins," she said. "Perhaps they were a memento of . . ."

Her voice trailed off, and I knew she was thinking about the mother she had never met. It was a romantic notion, that Volitar had kept that wealth secret, in memory of Zefra. It seemed to be a romantic story, what we knew of it. I knew Tarani believed she would meet her mother in Eddarta. I hoped, for Tarani's sake, that such a meeting would live up to her expectations.

"Volitar showed his love for Zefra in much more concrete ways, Tarani. I think he held on to those coins because spending them would be dangerous."

"But I have seen many Eddartan coins in Dyskornis, Rikardon."

"Gold twenty-*dozak* pieces? Bearing Pylomel's likeness?" I asked.

"I haven't seen many of the gold pieces, but . . . no, now that I think of it, I don't think I've ever seen coins like the ones we found with Zefra's letter. Do you think Volitar was afraid he could be traced here, if he spent the coins?"

I nodded.

"Then what shall *we* do with them?"

"Take them with us."

We were still in the marketplace, and just then I spotted a stall with leather goods and tanned, uncut skins.

"Here, hold these a minute," I said, and walked over to the leather dealer, who was seated under an awning supported by thin poles. On the ground around him were his wares. The worked goods—boots, belts, baldrics, vlek harnesses—were displayed on colored cloths. The skins—taken from *glith*, the deer-size food animal—were laid out in long lines, overlapped slightly so that a portion of each skin was visible. I walked around, bending over to look at the skins. When I found what I wanted, I sat down.

The dealer, who hadn't said a word (although he'd kept a wary eye on me), suddenly came to life.

"Yes, sir, how may I serve you this morning?"

I touched the glith skin I'd selected, asked him the price, and we started haggling.

"Sorry I took so long," I said, when I got back to Tarani with my new purchase. I took some of the bundles back, and we started walking northward, heading back to Volitar's shop. Tarani took the skin, which the dealer had rolled and tied, and looked it over skeptically.

"This is ugly," she said finally. "Thin and discolored—surely you could have afforded a better one. What are you going to do with it?"

At that moment, we were moving through the shopping crowd. "That's going to give me something to do along the way," I said. "Let's hurry, shall we? If we don't get back soon, Thymas is liable to leave without us."

She laughed at that, and I took pleasure in the sound of her laughter.

But I hadn't been far wrong. Thymas was waiting, with Ronar, at the downhill entrance to the living quarters attached to Volitar's shop. He had our saddlebags and backpacks laid out on the ground, open and ready for packing.

"Half the day is gone," he complained, reaching for the food parcels. "Is this all we're taking?"

"Put the food in the backpack, Thymas. You can put this—" I handed him the leather. "—in your bags with the cargo net. Tarani, if you don't mind, may we take some of Volitar's clothes along? And will you bring down the things in Volitar's chest?"

She paused at the door. "All of them?"

"Yes, the duplicate Ra'ira, too. Gharlas wanted it badly enough to kill Volitar for it. That makes it valuable to us." When she had gone in, I turned to Thymas.

"How are you doing—and tell me the truth."

He started to say something, stopped, and began again. "I still have some pain," he admitted.

Probably hurt you more to say that, *than your side hurts you,* I thought.

"Ronar will be suffering for a while, yet, too. To start out, Keeshah will carry Tarani and me, and the heavy supplies. You and Ronar can have both sets of sidebags, with the lighter stuff in them. We have three days of supplies here, and we're going to take all that time to get to the nearest town—Krasa, I think it is. We'll restock there. We'll stop when I say so. Agreed?"

"I've already agreed," he snapped. "How long before we'll reach Eddarta?"

"I figure it at around eighteen days—we should be a full seven-day ahead of Gharlas."

"And what then?" he demanded.

"I don't know yet," I said. "We have eighteen days to think about it. The more we rest, at the beginning, the greater our strength will be when we get there."

Thymas concentrated on his packing for a few seconds, then sat back and rubbed his hands across his trousers in a rare display of nervousness. But his voice was steady as he said: "A second rider is a strain for a sha'um during a long trip. When Ronar is feeling stronger, Tarani can ride with me half the time." He paused. "If she wants to." He paused again. "*Will* she want to?"

Tarani came out, carrying Volitar's chest in her hands, several tunics and trousers over one arm.

"Ask her, when the time comes," I said. "Now, let's get packed and on our way."

4

The map showed Krasa to be a little over six man-days—
I figured a man-day to be around thirty miles—away from
Dyskornis. In good health and at top speed, a sha'um
could cover the same distance in a third of a man's walking
time, but I had meant what I said to Thymas. We took it
easy, rising after dawn, camping well before night, and
taking long rests for the midday meal. Tarani put Thymas
and Ronar to sleep each night; Tarani, Keeshah, and I
shared the watch.

I might have relied on Keeshah's more efficient senses
to alert us to any danger, but I felt more comfortable with
a self-involved security plan.

You might say I was feeling paranoid.

Thanks to our noisy encounter with Gharlas and the
greedy thief who had tried to kill me, the entire rogueworld
of Dyskornis knew who I was. Worfit's reward for my
death, and the acquisition of Serkajon's steel sword, were
strong incentives for someone to follow us.

I was looking for danger up ahead, too. I believed we
were doing the right thing, or we wouldn't be doing it.
But the possibility that Gharlas *knew* what we were doing
was a constant worry, no matter how often I told myself
that worrying wouldn't solve anything.

Direct telepathy between Gandalarans was nearly unknown—but Gharlas said that the Ra'ira granted that power.
I had to believe him. He'd said he had learned about the
locked room where the Ra'ira was kept by reading Thanasset's

26

mind. He had known about Rikardon without being told—
I assumed that he had tried to read Markasset and had
sensed the change.

I was fairly sure that he *couldn't* read me, or Tarani. She
had proved in Dyskornis that her power could resist his.
But that didn't let out the possibility of his being able to
locate us, merely by the difference of our mind-patterns, or
whatever. And it didn't protect us from Gharlas reading
Thymas, who was more susceptible than either one of us.

So, useless as it was, I worried that Gharlas had traps
laid for us ahead.

But I didn't waste my time worrying. By the time we
reached Krasa, I had cut strips from the thin piece of
leather to fashion a belt. I worked the coins into the long
pocket one at a time; when no more would fit, we buried
the rest of them.

I was wearing that fortune in gold around my waist
when I walked into Krasa-to renew our supplies. The
weight was a burden at first, but it gave me a feeling of
satisfaction, that I had devised a way to conceal those
coins. I wasn't entirely sure why I felt it necessary to take
them to Eddarta, but I hadn't questioned the impulse.

We had left green, hilly forests behind in Eddarta, and
spent nearly two days in what I can only describe as scrub
brush—not quite desert, but close. As we neared Krasa,
the growth had turned green again, and I was walking
through a lightly overgrown forest. There were wild
dakathrenil here, the curly-trunked trees which, near
Raithskar, were trained to an umbrella shape slightly taller
than a man. Left to themselves, these wild ones sprawled
on the ground like woody vines.

There were other kinds of trees here, too, and a variety
of vines and flowers that I couldn't identify. I felt a familiar
frustration over Markasset's disinterest in anything besides
fighting, gambling, and Illia. This was a beautiful area, no
less dramatic because it stood close in the shadow of the
Great Wall.

I had already learned that the Great Wall was more or
less a convention of Gandalaran thinking. Behind Raithskar,

there was actually a *wall*—a sheer escarpment that vanished into overcast sky. Here, however, there were merely impassable mountains, and those not noticeably steeper than the Korchis west of Dyskornis. Yet these mountains were considered to be a continuation of Raithskar's barrier, and the Korchis a range of mountains.

I was learning to accept those conventions, just as I had accepted the physical aspects of my situation. My body wasn't human—*Homo sapiens* would have been desiccated in hours by the intense desert heat that I hardly noticed anymore. I could accept the fact that I would probably never find out *how* Ricardo had been transferred to this world. But there was one mystery that returned to plague me again and again: Where *was* Gandalara?

I took so many things for granted in Gandalara that I often wondered why I couldn't just let *this* mystery lie, why the question circled around at the back of my mind and popped up at idle moments. I supposed it was this world's physical character, and its intriguing similarities to, and differences from, Ricardo's earth.

The evolution of such similar species on two different worlds seemed impossible. It was coincidental, too, that Gandalara had a single moon and a twenty-eight-day lunar cycle. Yet Gandalara had too high levels of salt in its soil, and too little access to iron. And there was definitely *no* physical feature like the Great Wall anywhere in Ricardo's world.

Today I resolutely set aside the puzzle, so that I could enjoy my walk through the woods.

I heard a hooting call, and looked up to see Lonna, Tarani's bird companion, flying overhead. She swooped down and settled carefully on my shoulder, her big wings folding so that their tips crossed at the base of her tail. She was heavy, but I didn't mind—in fact, I was pleased that she had chosen me for company. I stroked the feathers on her breast as I walked, and she made a sound that was both mournful and contented.

You don't mind if I make a friend of Lonna, do you, Keeshah? I asked.

Girl is my friend, he pointed out, reminding me of a best-forgotten period of unrecognized jealousy. *Bird, too.*

Lonna left me when Krasa came into sight through the trees. It was a small town, built mostly of wood and baked clay—the sort of place where you're a stranger until your family has lived there for three generations.

I had all the supplies I planned to buy, and was leaving a bakery with fresh meat pastries, when someone behind me called my name.

"Rikardon?"

The voice wasn't familiar; the man it belonged to was walking toward me. He was short but stocky, with prominent supraorbital ridges, not much nose, and a whole lot of scars on his arms and face.

I had heard no threat in his voice, but I turned around and kept my hand near my sword as I answered.

"I am Rikardon. May I ask who you are?"

The scarred face creased into a smile. "You can ask me, or anyone in Krasa, son. My name is Ligor, and I'm what passes for the Chief of Peace and Security in this city. I have a message for you—from Zaddorn. And some free advice—from me. Join me for a drink?"

"Sure. How about that place on the corner?"

"Good choice," he said, and we moved along the packed-dirt surface of the street toward what Ricardo would have called a diner. It served light meals that could be eaten on the premises or taken outside, provided you left a deposit on the dishes. It also served *faen*, the Gandalaran equivalent of beer, as did almost every restaurant.

It was just past midday, and there was a late-lunch crowd keeping the help busy. The number of people surprised me, and I resolved never to judge a town by its appearance again. Krasa looked to be a pretty lively place.

Ligor caught the eye of one of the workers behind the service counter, and two earthenware mugs of faen appeared on a table at the back of the room, even before we could work our way through to it.

I was impressed.

"Zaddorn doesn't even know I'm in Krasa—yet," I said,

thinking of the message I had sent from Dyskornis. Thanasset would tell Zaddorn where I was, so that he wouldn't be expecting me any day, to fill the job he had offered me.

"True," Ligor said. He opened a pouch at his belt, and took out a fragile-looking letter. The thin paper had been folded umpteen times, obviously in order to be suitable for a maufa to carry it. "Read this," Ligor said. "Easier than my telling you."

I unfolded it, and leaned toward the window to get more light on the angular Gandalaran characters.

> *Ligor, old friend, I need your help. A caravan master named Gharlas stole something important, something you'll recognize if you see it. He's a dangerous man, and it's imperative that he be stopped before he reaches Eddarta. I doubt that he'll come by your way, but if you hear anything at all of his movements, please let me know.*
>
> *There's another person you might encounter, a fellow named Rikardon. You'll recognize him, too—you knew him as Markasset. He left Raithskar today, and he may be following Gharlas. If you see him, trust him and help him all you can. And tell him, for me, that he's got the job, like it or not. I'm telling all my contacts to give him full cooperation.*

Terrific, I thought. *Now I'm a deputy sheriff.*

"So this is the message," I said. "Now what's the advice?"

"Just this, son. Don't rely on any of that help he promised. Zaddorn doesn't know anything about this side of the world."

"How do you know Zaddorn? And—I'm sorry, but I don't remember you."

"Not much reason you should. It was always Zaddorn tagging after me, not the Supervisor's son." He took a sip of his faen. "I used to have Zaddorn's job."

"He mentioned he took office just after Ferrathyn succeeded Bromer as Chief Supervisor."

"Yeah. Ferrathyn fired me."

30

I searched Markasset's memory for Raithskarian law. "He couldn't do that himself, could he?"

"No, it was all proper, with unanimous approval of the Council. But it was Ferrathyn who started it. I bear no grudge, mind you—it wasn't just because the old man and I didn't get on well, though that was for sure true. Mostly it was because I didn't fit the Peace and Security image the Council wanted for Raithskar. I did my job, but I didn't do it..."

He struggled to find the right word, and I provided one that seemed to fit: "Gracefully."

He laughed and slapped the table. "That's it, exactly."

"I didn't mean—"

"Don't worry about it, son. I know what I am, and what I'm not. Graceful, I'm not. I've got a lot of blunt edges. Zaddorn's a good man, keen as a sword. He cuts cleanly what I'd bruise to death.

"But, to get back to that free advice, he's got his limitations, too. One is, he trusts too much."

"Zaddorn?"

"Oh, not people in general. Nobody works in our business without getting to be naturally suspicious of everybody. But he thinks every Peace Officer is respected, and has the kind of authority he has, with the Council to back him up."

"And you're telling me he's wrong?"

Ligor lifted his empty mug, and the same waiter appeared to refill both our drinks. The crowd was thinning out, and we could converse more comfortably.

"I'm telling you just that. He has his little list of Peace and Security Officers, and he writes to them, and he expects them all to be as conscientious and powerful as he is. He's got a security force of better than two hundred men. How many men you think I got working for me?"

I didn't have to think hard; he'd already telegraphed the answer. "None," I said, and he nodded.

"And I'm one of the good guys, the ones who try. Zaddorn's other 'contacts'—some of them have moved, or they're dead. Some of them might try to stop Gharlas, all

31

right. They've got their own 'contacts' that can sell any . . . *important* thing they might find on his body."

"Say it straight, Ligor," I said, a little impatiently.

"All right. What Zaddorn did, with letters like this," he tapped the parchment I still held in my hand, "is warn the whole countryside that you're on your way to Eddarta. Stay away from those Peace and Security people. If they cooperate with anybody, it will be Worfit."

"The reward." In a flash vision, I saw the bloody face of the man who had tried to kill me for that same reward. I remembered the resistance against my sword as its blade passed through his body. I closed my eyes to block the vision.

After a moment, Ligor said: "You still going?"

"To Eddarta? Yes." I drained my mug, stood up, and reached for my pouch. He put his hand out to stop me.

"No, you're my guest, son. Free food and faen are part of my wages. I don't often stand host; there aren't many folk around that I'd care to drink with. Zaddorn is one. Now there are two." He stood up, slapped my arm, and gripped it for a moment. "Stay alive, boy. I'm looking forward to our next drink together."

5

I'm not paranoid, I thought. *Everybody really is out to get me.*

It was the second morning after my talk with Ligor. We were camped within walking range of Grevor, and Thymas had just now left, on his way into town. I wouldn't say his exit had been graceful. "Snarly" might describe it better.

"What is *wrong* with him?" Tarani demanded. She was standing in the middle of the clearing, staring after the boy. "His body gets better, and his temper gets worse. Surely he knows the walk will help him." She put her hands on her hips and looked speculatively at me. "You know, don't you? What *is* wrong?"

I shrugged. "He didn't believe a word I said."

"It made perfect sense to me," she said. "I think you are right about Gharlas—if he left traps for us, I would be his main target. And your friend in Krasa warned you that every town has been alerted to watch for you. So Thymas is the only one left who can get supplies. How can he not agree with that reasoning?"

"I didn't say that he didn't see the logic of the arguments," I answered. "He wouldn't have gone at all, in that case. What I mean is, he doesn't believe that any of that covers the real reason why I wanted him to go into town this time."

"Then what *does* he think?" she asked.

Can she really not know? I wondered. *Sometimes she's twenty, going on forty-five, and other times she's so naive . . .*

"That I wanted to be alone with you."

33

"That's ridiculous," she snorted. "You *are* alone with me, every night. There's nothing much that can wake him, once he's in the healing sleep."

"Maybe that's what's bothering him," I said.

She stared at me in confusion for the space of a heartbeat, then blushed clear up to her widow's peak of dark, silky headfur. "Perhaps," she said, sounding dangerous, "we should have a talk, the three of us, when Thymas returns."

"Ordinarily, I'd say that was a good idea. But not this time. His jealousy is only part of what's causing his mood, Tarani. The main thing is that he isn't *in control* of any aspect of this situation. He can't make his body heal any faster. He agreed to take my orders, but he doesn't much like doing it. He hates seeing you ride with me, but he knows you have to until Ronar gets stronger. And he can't hurry that along, either."

Tarani's arms dropped to her sides, and her eyes snapped wide open. "You mean that he will *let* me ride with him? That Ronar will accept me?"

"He said as much, before we left Dyskornis. I believe him. But he did seem to have some doubt as to whether you'd want to ride with him."

"Want to? Of course I do." She stopped, then fumbled on. "I mean—Keeshah could use the rest."

I smiled, and said: "Don't back away from it, Tarani."

She recognized the quote, and suddenly started to laugh. "All right, then, we shall be honest with one another. How will you feel, when I ride with Thymas?"

I sighed. "Jealous," I admitted. She laughed again, then sobered when I threw her question back to her: "How will you feel?"

She thought about it before she answered. "Proud that Thymas would accept me. Pleased for him, that he could make such a major change in his thinking. And I suppose I would feel . . . close to him. Do you understand?"

"I think so," I said.

It's ironic, really, I thought, *that Thymas is jealous of me. Riding may involve a lot of physical contact, but with me, it can only stimulate Tarani's imagination. With him, it will bring back memories. That gives him an edge I can't hope to overcome.*

Keeshah, I called. *Feel like going for a run?*

Both? he asked.

No, just me.

He came out of the forest, shaking his head as an ear brushed against a low branch. Tarani went to him and stroked the fur along his cheek. He put up with it for only a few seconds before pulling away and crouching to let me mount.

I thought for a moment that Tarani felt insulted. Then she smiled, and I decided I must have been mistaken.

"I can see that I'm not the one you want to yourself, Rikardon."

I sat down on Keeshah's back, and he stood up. "I'll be back soon," I promised. "Keeshah's itching for a run; that's all."

She said: "I understand."

I lay forward and grabbed the fur on either side of the cat's wide shoulders, and I tucked up my legs so that my feet rested just in front of his haunches. It felt strange, riding without the warm weight of Tarani's body across my back.

She can come too, Keeshah told me, sensing, as usual, the undercurrent of my feelings for Tarani.

I don't want her this time, I said, and hoped he would accept it. *Do you?*

No. Tired of walking. Want to RUN.

And he did.

At first, we crashed through trees and jumped over tangled brush, but it wasn't long before we were out in the near-desert that lurked at the edge of every watered area along the Great Wall. Then I reached out for Keeshah's mind, and we were one entity, pounding across the grayish sand on the sha'um's enormous paws.

The rhythm of his movement was as much a part of me as my own pulse. He felt the wind sweeping at me, and the way his fur felt against my cheek. It was a raw and

35

natural and savage pleasure, the joy we shared when we ran together like this. When we returned to camp—much later than I had planned—we were both exhausted and exhilarated.

I hugged the big cat good-bye some distance from camp, and walked the rest of the way. I felt more relaxed than I had since the days I had spent in Thagorn, getting to know the Sharith lifestyle. Lonna greeted me, and I shouted a "hello" back at her.

Thymas had returned from Grevor, with fresh food for dinner. That—and the fact that he looked as though his walk had done him good—completed the good feeling that the run had kindled in me. After dinner, we discussed travel plans.

"The old couple who ran the meat shop said that there's a colony of vineh between here and Sulis," Thymas said.

"Wild ones?" I asked.

"Are there any other kind?"

Tarani's question was serious, and I realized that neither she nor Thymas had ever been to Raithskar. So I told them about the vineh who swept streets and paved roads and did other, fairly simple jobs under the supervision of their handlers. Tarani and Thymas looked skeptical.

"Why would I lie about it?" I asked.

"It's just that I can't imagine a trainable vineh," Thymas said. "Have you ever seen a wild one?"

"Not really," I answered, thinking of the scuffle I had witnessed in the streets of Raithskar, where a handler had almost gotten mauled by three of the curly haired, apish creatures. "What are they like?"

"Just hope you don't find out," Thymas said. "They said that this colony has a live-and-let-live attitude, *if* travelers stick to the road while they're crossing vineh territory. Anyplace off the road is a battle zone."

There was a problem with traveling the road. We were trying to keep the sha'um out of sight, and we didn't know how well traveled the road between Sulis and Grevor was. Thymas said that vineh denned in caves, so we decided to swing out south of the road and avoid their territory altogether.

It turned out to be pretty rough country, with lots of ground-hugging bushes that hid the actual contours of the land. But for this day only, I agreed to hurry. I glanced at Thymas and Ronar now and then, and was glad to see that they were handling the pace pretty well. In fact, I was looking back at them when the vineh attacked.

There were at least twenty of them, clawing their way out of an overgrown ravine and coming straight for us. There weren't any young ones, either; these were adult males, taller than a Gandalaran, at least as strong, with no sense of reason to which we might appeal.

They were out to get us.

In Ricardo's world, a mounted man had an advantage over infantry in that he could strike from above. But in Ricardo's world, the cavalry wasn't riding sha'um.

I can recall a second or two of the wildest ride I've ever had, as Keeshah roared his challenge, leaped forward, and slashed and snapped at the nearest four vineh. Then Tarani and I were left behind, rolling on the ground.

A vineh thudded down on top of me, his hands pulling at my head and shoulder to get room for his underslung jaw to close on my throat. I curled up, got my knees under his hips, and pushed. I couldn't throw him off, but I managed to lift him enough to get my hands around his throat. His neck was so thick, the muscles so strong, that for a minute I was afraid I couldn't hurt him at all. Then my right thumb found a soft spot and dug in.

The beast made a strangling sound and grabbed my arms to stop the choking. I heaved with my legs; we rolled a couple of times, and I came out on top. Using the vineh's throat as a pivot, I jumped up and brought both knees down on his chest. I felt a rib crack, and the beast's eyes went glassy.

I drew my dagger and finished him, just as a hairy arm grabbed me around the throat and jerked, nearly twisting my head off. The pain and lack of air canceled out my eyesight, and I saw the swirling, undefined colors of unconsciousness closing in on me.

The pressure was released suddenly, and I could breathe. When my vision cleared, I saw Tarani pulling her sword out of a vineh's back. I got Rika up in time to stop another one from attacking her from behind.

"Where's Thymas?" I gasped.

"Over there." She tossed her head, then whirled to face a vineh who was trying to rush her from the side.

I looked in the direction she had indicated. Thymas had backed into the rocks, so that he stood in a shallow passage, and a frontal attack was the only kind possible. With sword and dagger, he was managing to hold off three vineh, but he was leaning to his right, to protect his wounded side, and his face was already gray with fatigue.

"*Rikardon!*" Tarani warned me. I ducked down and caught the running vineh across the middle with my shoulder. I intended to flip him over my back, but he was too heavy and my balance wasn't perfect, so we went down together, grappling. But I had knocked the wind from him; he didn't fight me as I used my dagger. Tarani guarded me as I stood up, and we discovered that we were alone among the fighting. Except for the three vineh keeping Thymas at bay, the rest of them were in two great snarling and snapping crowds roiling around the sha'um.

Keeshah was holding his own, whirling so quickly that the vineh were forced to keep their distance. But Ronar was slower, and the vineh were applying their favorite trick of attacking from behind. Even as we stood there, we saw four vineh converge on the cat's flanks. Ronar screamed in rage as teeth sank into his hindquarters, and he rolled over to get his hind claws into play.

Immediately, all ten or twelve vineh jumped the cat, trying to immobilize him with the sheer weight of their bodies. Tarani and I ran to help, leaping across the ring of dead beasts to harry the outer layer of Ronar's attackers. The vineh were so frenzied with the prospect of victory over the sha'um that they didn't notice us until we had killed two apiece. Then they turned and rushed us. Through

38

the forest of curly haired bodies, I saw Ronar stagger to his feet. Clearly, he was close to exhaustion, but he lashed out at the nearest vineh, opening claw-gashes three inches deep across the beast's back.

Tarani and I tried to retreat, but the tangle of bodies provided unstable, blood-slick footing, and within seconds, we were surrounded.

It wasn't the first time I had reason to be grateful for the Gandalaran body I had "inherited." Young and fit, Markasset had been an expert swordsman, and his reflexes took over in times of physical danger. But I know I'd never have survived, that day, without Tarani to guard my back.

That's one I owe you, Thymas, I thought. *Thanks for teaching this woman to fight.*

With Ronar's help, we reduced our attack group to five vineh. But Serkajon's sword was getting heavier by the minute, and my hands didn't want to hold on to it. Tarani seemed in as poor a shape as I felt; her clothes were bloody, her movements slowing.

The vineh who faced us now had been at the outer edge of the fighting, and were nearly fresh. They started closing in on us, and I knew we were in trouble. Worse, *they* knew it.

But Keeshah sensed it, too. He clawed his way through the three or four still dogging him, and launched himself, four sets of claws ready, at the group coming after us.

Once Keeshah, Tarani, and I were working together, it penetrated to the remaining vineh that they weren't winning.

It took long enough, I thought, as the seven or eight survivors scrambled back into the ravine. *We've been fighting for at least a year.*

I wanted to lie down and sleep, but there were other things to do first. I found Thymas in the rock niche where we had seen him fighting. He was hunched over and nearly unconscious.

"I think he's all right," I called to Tarani. "Scratched up pretty badly, but alive."

I hauled him up to his feet and put his arm around my shoulders. Tarani was trying to tend to Ronar, who was

39

bleeding badly but too much in pain and shock to let her touch him. Thymas couldn't help control him—in fact, his dazed state was probably communicating itself to Ronar.

Keeshah, he has to lie down, or Tarani can't help him.

Keeshah's neck fur was still bristling from the excitement of the fight. Thymas's sha'um bristled and snarled in an automatic defense reflex when mine closed in, but couldn't offer much resistance. Keeshah wrestled Ronar to the ground and lay across his shoulders to keep him still while Tarani cleaned the deepest gashes on the cat's flanks.

I lowered Thymas to the ground and tended him as best I could. He was coming around by the time Tarani got up from Ronar and came over to us.

When Keeshah moved off of him, Ronar rolled up into a crouch and lay there panting. Keeshah cleaned himself—his wounds were mere scratches—and then worked his raspy tongue across the fur on Ronar's back, licking away the dirt and blood. He was careful not to disturb the ointment Tarani had applied to Ronar's flanks.

"We need to rest for a couple of days," I said, watching the sha'um. "But not here. Thymas, can Ronar walk?"

He closed his eyes for a moment, speaking to the great cat. "Yes. But not far." His hand, pitifully weak, closed on my arm. "This time, Rikardon, you don't have a choice. You have to leave us behind."

"You may be right, Thymas," I said, reluctantly. "But we still have a safety margin for beating Gharlas to Eddarta. We can afford a couple of slow days. If we *do* have to go on without you, at least we can leave you in a more hospitable place."

6

He didn't have the energy to argue. In fact, he'd been pushing his own and Ronar's reserves to keep up with the morning's fast pace. Now man and sha'um both were drained, physically and psychologically.

Ronar could barely walk; there was no question of Thymas riding him. I considered asking Keeshah to carry the Sharith boy, so that Tarani and I could keep our swords ready for another attack, but rejected the idea before it really took shape. Keeshah might not have objected—but it would have been a mortal blow to Ronar's pride, which was already down for the count. So Tarani and I traded off supporting Thymas while we all three walked, nervously, eastward toward Sulis. Keeshah circled warily around us and Lonna kept a lookout from the sky.

Thymas's informant had said the vineh lived "between Grevor and Sulis," so we couldn't be sure of being safe until we had actually reached the next town.

We didn't find it before nightfall. We took a brief rest, and Tarani asked Lonna to locate the town for us.

The bird reported that Sulis was close, and the way was fairly clear, so we dragged our weary bodies up once again and plodded on. We stopped just outside the city to find a concealed place for the sha'um to rest. Weary as she was, Tarani took the time to hum Ronar to sleep.

I will guard, and hunt, Keeshah told me. *This one will have meat at dawn; then I will rest.*

41

Good, Keeshah, I said. *We will all rest for a day, at least.*

Privately I thought: *They've come a long way—from fighting one another to taking care of each other.* I looked down at Thymas. Tarani's sleep spell had unintentionally zapped him, too. *But then,* I thought, pulling Thymas up from the ground and getting my shoulders under him, *Thymas and I are making the same kind of progress.*

I groaned as I lifted him. He wasn't as tall as Tarani, who was nearly eye-to-eye with me, but every inch of him was solid, hard-packed muscle. Thymas was a hefty chunk.

"Can you manage him alone?" Tarani asked, steadying me as I staggered a little.

"For a while, anyway," I grunted.

If Sulis had been one step further away, I wouldn't have made it. As it was, I stumbled into an inn and dumped Thymas on the registration table. The startled clerk didn't have to ask what had happened to us, but he was plainly curious about how we had survived an encounter with vineh.

"We *won't* survive, if we don't get some rest," Tarani said. "Will you help us take our friend to our room?"

"One room for the three of you?" the clerk asked, then seemed to realize that the question might be offensive. "That is—"

"*Yes*, one room for the three of us," Tarani said. "Please hurry."

It cost us the rest of our non-Eddartan cash, but that was the best night's sleep I ever had.

I didn't move until nearly noon the next day, and even though I was stiff and sore, thanks to the vineh and the strain of carrying Thymas, I woke up feeling confident.

Tarani and Thymas were still sleeping. I slid a single gold coin from my belt and went out of the room quietly. We'd need to eat, sometime between Sulis and Eddarta, and the Eddartan coins were now our only choice. We'd have to risk their being identified. I went in search of a moneychanger.

The man I found had never seen a coin exactly like it,

and offered the opinion that it had been stamped to commemorate some occasion. But he shrugged and said: "Gold is gold, no matter whose face it wears." After he had taken his commission for changing the twenty-*dozak* piece, I had two hundred and thirty-eight *zaks*, in assorted coin sizes, available for spending. It was enough, easily, to manage the rest of the trip—depending on what I decided to do with Thymas.

He was going to have to stay behind and follow later; that much was clear. The exertion of the fight with the vineh had pushed both him and Ronar back to "square one", in terms of their recovering stamina and spirit.

Keeshah had to come with me, or our plan of laying some kind of trap in Eddarta before Gharlas got there would be useless. But Tarani—did *she* have to come with me?

I mulled over the possible choices as I sat in the inn's dining room, sipping faen.

One, she could come with me, and leave Thymas to follow whenever he and Ronar could travel. Would Thymas wait until they were recovered? Or would he be just as heedlessly anxious to get going as he had been in Dyskornis, and arrive in Eddarta too weak to be any help at all? Worse than that, would he let his depression convince him that he might as well not follow at all?

Two, Tarani could stay with Thymas, so that he and Ronar would heal faster. Ronar would travel more slowly, carrying double, but they would be able to leave sooner.

I hate it, I thought, *but the second choice makes more sense. Are there any reasons why Tarani shouldn't stay behind with Thymas? Real reasons, that is—not jealous ones.*

There *was* one reason. Zefra.

I had considered Tarani's plan to find her mother as secondary to our need to find the Ra'ira. But if we could find Zefra, it was possible that she could *help* us against Gharlas.

If *Tarani* asked her.

I paid for my drink, and went upstairs to tell Tarani and Thymas what I had decided.

They didn't question it—Thymas would stay; Tarani would go. The only argument I got was, predictably, from Thymas.

"You will lose time if you move me elsewhere," he protested. "There is game here for Ronar, and I can rest here just as well as anywhere else. Pay the clerk for a few days of room and board, and go!"

"I *will not* leave you here, Thymas," I said. "You need experienced care, and a lot of rest. If you stayed here, you'd be on your guard all the time. We'll take you to a Refreshment House; you'll be safe with the Fa'aldu." I spread out the map, studied it for a moment, then tapped it with my finger. "Stomestad."

"Too far," Thymas snapped. "You'd lose three days, poking along at our speed."

"It would be straight across desert," Tarani mused. "A rough trip."

"We can stand a few days of desert travel," I said. "And Stomestad lies along the most direct route to Eddarta from here. Even if Tarani and I can't make up the lost time, we should still be able to reach Eddarta before Gharlas gets there. We'll go to Stomestad."

I was expecting desert, but not *that* desert. It made the Kapiral, with its stubborn, ground-hugging dry bushes, seem like paradise. *Nothing* grew in that wasteland. The air felt superheated, and the sand was so fine that we had to wrap our faces to keep from inhaling salty particles drifting in the air like dust motes.

By the time I realized what we were getting into, it was the middle of our second day, and too late to turn back. We adopted the travel pattern I had learned from Zaddorn: move for three hours, rest for one, the three of us hugging the shadows of the sha'um. Healthy sha'um could have run the trip from Sulis to Stomestad in two and a half days. It took us five days and nights of miserable tramping before we arrived at the symbolic canvas barrier of Stomestad.

It was mid-afternoon, and the sand shifted under our feet as we stood there, croaking the ritual request for shelter. Vasklar, Respected Elder of the Refreshment House, granted our request and ordered that the symbolic canvas barrier be lowered to admit us. He stared at us in shock for a moment, then hurried his people to help us.

The Refreshment House of Stomestad was the largest I had yet seen. It was enclosed in the same way as all the others I had visited, with a head-high wall of large bricks of rock salt. The interior compound, where the extended family group of desert dwellers lived, seemed much larger than those I had seen at Yafnaar and Relenor.

The Fa'aldu provided most travelers with sparing accommodations—mere cubicles with sleeping ledges and plain pallets. The small rooms opened directly on the enclosed courtyard where, on any given night, there might be twenty to a hundred vleks stamping and bawling. Travelers were also given water and cooked food, all in trade for some kind of goods—food products, fabric, crafted articles.

Across the long, rectangular court were doorways which opened into the family residence area.

I was one of the few travelers ever invited into the Fa'aldu homes—a privilege for which I often thanked Balgokh, the Elder at Yafnaar, who had been Ricardo's first source of information in Gandalara. Balgokh didn't know the truth about me; he believed that Markasset had awakened in the desert without his memory, and had later regained it. He had taken a fatherly pride in my possession of Serkajon's sword, and had accepted, without question, Thanasset's decision to implement the old custom of changing a son's name when he has proved himself ready to carry the family's sword.

It was part of the obligation of the Fa'aldu, assumed during the time of the Kingdom, to assist anyone in need in the desert. But I thought that Balgokh had helped me willingly, because he had sensed something of my difference from other Gandalarans. So I had returned to Yafnaar to give him a resolution to the mystery I had started.

Balgokh had appreciated that gesture so much that he had sent word to all the Refreshment Houses, asking that I be honored as a fellow Fa'aldu.

And, as a side effect, making me into a legend.

When we surrendered our weapons and gave our names, the whole family came out to help.

The respect of the Stomestad Fa'aldu embarrassed me, but I didn't hesitate to take advantage of it. Fa'aldu children dusted us off with stiff-bristled brushes, and gave us a little water. Then Tarani took Thymas into a cubicle to tend him, while I arranged for meat and water for the sha'um, and had a talk with Vasklar.

Thymas's wounds, though deeper and nastier looking than the bruises and scratches Tarani and I had suffered, had been reduced to thin scabs after the two nights he spent in Sulis under Tarani's healing sleep, but the trek across the desert had reopened some of the worse ones. The salty grit that covered us from head to foot had crusted in the bloody scars, even though we had used some of our precious water to clean them whenever we rested. The edges of the opened wounds looked swollen and inflamed, even after they had been cleansed.

I went into Thymas's cubicle just as Tarani was using the last of her supply of soothing ointment on Thymas's nastiest gash. It started beneath his right ear, and slid down his neck and across the right side of his chest. She was sitting on the sleeping ledge with her back to me, blocking sight of Thymas's face, but I could see most of his body. She left her hands on his chest after she finished, moving them in small circles, massaging lightly. He said something too softly for me to hear it, and she laughed.

"I need to talk to Thymas for a minute," I said. She jumped, then stood up and left the room, turning back once to smile at the boy.

"I guess you know that Ronar is doing pretty well," I said, sitting down where Tarani had been. I could feel her warmth in the thin padding of the pallet, even on the surface of the huge block of rock salt beneath it. Thymas watched me warily, waiting. "Tarani's ointment matted his fur over those really bad cuts, and kept out the dust. They're starting to heal. I want you to stay here until you both feel *fit* to travel—got that?"

The boy nodded, and winced with the pain the motion cost him.

"Tarani will help you and Ronar sleep tonight—that should give you a good start on getting well. Vasklar will take good care of you, and he will give you whatever provisions you need when you're ready to go. Wait until Ronar can travel full speed, and ride directly for Eddarta."

"Where will you be?" he asked.

"Tarani and Keeshah and I will leave in the morning for the Refreshment House of Iribos. Vasklar gave me the name of one of the Fa'aldu there who can tell us about Eddarta. When we have some kind of a plan, Tarani will send Lonna to you with the details. If you need to contact us, send Lonna back—she'll be able to find Tarani, no matter where we are."

"All right," he sighed, and closed his eyes. There were creases of weariness radiating from their corners.

"One more thing, and I'll let you get some rest," I said.

He opened his eyes and looked at me again. I didn't have a clue as to what he was thinking.

"I'm going to leave Serkajon's sword here, where it will be safe, and where it can't identify me. I'll take yours in its place."

He didn't say anything, and after a second or two, I stood up.

"See you in Eddarta," I said, and went out into the courtyard.

I had supper with Vasklar's family, but Tarani had declined their invitation, pleading fatigue. The Refreshment House wasn't crowded, so Vasklar had given each of us a separate sleeping room. As I crossed the lamp-lit courtyard, I noticed light around the edges of the tapestry hanging which served as a door to Thymas's room.

Tarani said she was going to eat, put Thymas to sleep, and then get some sleep, herself, I remembered. *It's late—she probably left the lamp burning by accident.*

47

I stepped to the door and pulled aside the curtain. Tarani was seated in the same place; I couldn't see her face, or Thymas's. But as I watched, too startled to move, his hand touched her arm and moved along it slowly until he was holding her shoulder. She leaned forward, and both of his arms embraced her.

I dropped the curtain and moved away quietly.

7

"We're here," I said to Tarani, who had been struggling along stubbornly against her weariness, staring at the ground. We had left Keeshah where desert and the far end of a branch of the Tashal River merged to form a treacherous salt bog. For two days, we had walked through farmland. With every step, I had been forced to revise my impression of the size of Eddarta. A city which needed this much produce to feed its people must include a sizable collection of individuals.

Tarani's head lifted, and together we stared at the huge, strange city. Following the directions we had been given, we were approaching from the northwest along a well-traveled road that bordered the westernmost branch of the river. After many intersections, this road would lead us into the city—or, rather into *part* of the city.

There were two Eddartas. The original, older city sprawled on the lower slopes of the River Wall and drifted out toward the fields in strings and clumps of tiny buildings. Several branches of the Tashal flowed and rushed through the city itself, and the largest streets followed along beside them. All those wide boulevards merged into a paved avenue that led uphill to the second Eddarta.

This was a stone-walled enclosure entirely separate from what I had already begun to think of as "lower" Eddarta. Its only links to the bigger town were the steep avenue and a single branch of the Tashal which meandered along the upper city's level, but tumbled in sparkling cataracts

49

above and below it. The lower rapids came straight down the hill, beside the entry avenue.

"I didn't expect it to be so large," Tarani said, after a moment.

"Neither did I," I admitted. "But remember, we already know where to find the people we want to see."

"Inside those walls," Tarani said. There was no awe, or fear, just the statement. I knew she was thinking about her mother, but she said: "Do you think we have arrived before Gharlas?"

"Unless he learned how to fly these past three days, we're at least two days ahead of him. But just in case . . . do you think you can disguise us until we're safely in Yoman's shop? He said that guards are along the roads to check people going *out*, but if Gharlas sent word ahead . . ."

"I can do it," she said. "Before we approach the guards, we will need to move off the road, out of sight, for a moment. Then stay very close to me; it will be harder if we are separated."

A quarter of an hour later, the road turned to follow a branch of the river. Its banks were lined with tall, reedy plants, and Tarani stepped into the concealment they offered. I waited a moment, then followed her. We stepped out together.

When I looked at Tarani, I could see the illusion she cast for herself—the pale-haired, rounded body of Rassa. I could see Tarani through it, as though the image of Rassa were only a transparent hologram, but I was sure that everyone else who looked directly at Tarani, would see only Rassa. I assumed that I would pass for Yoman.

We had met those two people at the Refreshment House of Iribos, after explaining what we needed to the person Vasklar had named. I had been astonished to learn that our Iribos contact and Vasklar were both involved in providing an escape route for Eddartan slaves. It was strictly in violation of the noninterference rules of the Fa'aldu, but I had commended their courage.

Yoman and Rassa weren't slaves, but craftsmen—clothing designers, specifically. They were "free" to work for pay, as

50

long as they turned over a high percentage of their profit to the Lord who owned the property on which their shop was located.

It appealed strongly to Tarani that they had tired of their life in Eddarta, and decided to escape from it, much as Volitar had escaped years ago. How they had known whom to contact in Iribos was a mystery, but arrangements had been made for them to be "registered" with a caravan leaving the following day. Pylomel had informants everywhere, it seemed, who were on the lookout for unattached people who might be wanted in Eddarta. Such informants undoubtedly had been responsible for Zefra's identification in Dyskornis.

We had found it necessary to reveal Tarani's skill at illusion. After our contact recovered from the shock, the two Eddartans had been brought to us. They represented an opportunity to enter Eddarta without question. Tarani and I would have a place to stay, and real identities to conceal us.

Yoman, who was as tall as I, middle-aged, with a touch of softness around his stomach, had assured me that their short absence could be explained easily as a trip to visit an ill relative, should anyone inquire. He had given us that, and other, information in response to our questions, and he had volunteered little else.

Rassa, his daughter, had said nothing at all. She was a physical type that Tarani could imitate easily. As tall as Tarani, she had the same smooth brow and delicate planes at cheek and jaw. It was obvious that the two women shared some genes. But where Tarani's headfur was black and silky, Rassa's was thick and golden. Body curves at breast and hip were more pronounced in Rassa, and she walked with an unconscious sensuality that wasn't damaged at all by her haunting beauty.

Yoman and Rassa had become our key to Eddarta, and we had sent Lonna to Thymas with instructions to look for us at Yoman's tailor shop when he reached Eddarta. But I was uneasy as we walked within Tarani's illusion. I couldn't rid myself of the feeling that the merchant had been holding something back, that he had been running from Eddarta for a reason more specific than weariness of his lifestyle.

I didn't want to be recognized as Rikardon. But I was halfway expecting some hassle when I was recognized as Yoman.

That danger didn't materialize, much to my relief. A couple of people said hello, but in the crowded streets, with folks hurrying to get home before dark, there wasn't time to do much more than wave and smile. By the time we located Yoman's shop, staggered through the doors and closed them behind us, I was a bundle of exposed nerves.

"Who is it? Who is there?" The quavering voice came from a man at the top of a flight of stairs that ended just to our right. He was silhouetted against a small window which let in some light from the street lamps below. He was a small man, and looked frail. He was wearing only a pair of trousers, tied with drawstrings at waist and ankles, and I could see the outline of his ribs.

I squeezed Tarani's hand. "He can't see us. Can you give me Yoman's voice?" I whispered. She returned the pressure, and I cleared my throat loudly.

"Who am I? Yoman, that's who! Now who are you, in my shop this time of night?"

"Yoman?" the voice whined. "Yoman, it is Bress, your good friend! Wait, I'll get a lamp . . ."

Bress. Yoman mentioned him—another fabric merchant.

"Bress!" I bellowed. "I need no lamp to see what is going on here! I am gone a few days, and you move in to take over my shop!" I started up the stairs, stomping heavily. The skinny old man whimpered with fright.

"No, I moved in here to *protect* your shop, Yoman! I didn't know where you had gone—someone else might have—"

I was near the top of the stairs, drawing Tarani up right behind me. The old man was holding a lamp base and struggling with a scissor-shaped sparker.

"No one else needed to," I yelled, causing the little guy to drop the bronze platform onto the hallway table. The fall jarred the glass chimney, which had been set aside, off balance; it toppled, rolled off the table, and made a nerve-jangling noise as it shattered. Bress jumped two feet into the air and completely lost his nerve.

"Please, Yoman, I meant no harm. You went away and left no word, you know how small my shop is, we have been friends, I didn't want them to think it was abandoned—"

"Out!" I said. I grabbed one thin arm and propelled the man toward the stairs, turning Tarani behind me to keep her hidden. "And be thankful you still have your head. Rassa and I have traveled a long, hard way this day. Anything you moved *in*, you can move *out* tomorrow."

The little man dived halfway down the stairs, clutched at the railing to save himself, and stumbled the rest of the way. At the door, he paused to look up. I could barely see him.

"Rassa is with you?" he said in surprise. "But I thought surely..." I took the first step down, and he hurriedly opened the door. "No matter, Yoman, it's none of my affair. But—I do mean this, my friend—I *am* glad you've come to your senses. All we heard were rumors, remember." He ducked out the door.

I wonder what he meant by that? I thought, as I turned back to Tarani—just in time to see her start to fall.

"Tarani!" I whispered, as I caught her under her arms and tried, clumsily, to disentangle her from the backpack. She was limp against my chest, a dead weight that was almost too much for me to handle.

The illusions did it, I told myself. *On top of all that physical exertion, the psychic strain was too much. Why the hell didn't she tell me? Damn it, if she's pushed herself too far...*

I finally freed the backpack and dropped it to the floor. She had slipped down until she was nearly on her knees, and I was badly off balance. I was beginning to worry that I'd topple over backward and drag us both down the stairs, when she moved a little and clutched at my waist. I helped her as she pulled herself to her feet.

"Sorry," she murmured, still half-dazed. "I'll be all right soon—"

"A good night's sleep won't hurt you any," I said gruffly, as I lifted her in my arms. "Let's see if we can find Rassa's bedroom."

Cradled against my chest, Tarani's weight was manageable. It was relief, not fear of dropping her, that made my arms hold her so tightly.

I knelt down and laid her on the fluffy pallet in the smaller of the two bedrooms.

She propped herself on one elbow as I sat down beside her. There were two windows in this room, open to the night. The faint starlight, and stray beams from street lamps, gave us enough light to see each other. Her face, always delicate, looked fragile in the gray light.

"Why didn't you warn me that the illusions of Yoman and Rassa would cost you so dearly?"

"I didn't know," she said. "I've never tried to sustain an illusion for such a long period of time."

"Or for someone else?" I asked.

"Yes, that was a factor, too."

"You could have told me, when you felt the strain," I said, trying not to sound like I was accusing her.

"In Dyskornis, you said we had to be able to depend on one another, Rikardon. I had said I could hold the illusion; I had to see it through."

She only did what I'd have done, myself, I admitted. *Except that I couldn't have done it at all. Which is why she's here, isn't it? She's right—I can't preach teamwork and then tell one of the players not to do her part.*

"I can't argue with that," I said, and started to get up. Her free hand caught my arm and I paused, kneeling very close to her.

"Rikardon, your caring . . . it touches me deeply."

I felt the world shifting and changing around me.

The image of Tarani and Thymas together had burned itself in my memory, and I saw it again now, but with a different perspective. Then, and on the following nights, the remembered scene had seemed confirmation of Tarani's

54

continuing affection for Thymas, and I had kept myself a scrupulous distance from the girl, especially in my thoughts as we rode together.

But there was no mistaking the invitation in her voice and posture, and another scene rose vividly in memory— the evening we had talked in Dyskornis and, in the most cautious of language, admitted the attraction we felt for one another. The scene in Stomestad was driven out of my memory. Tarani was with me, here and now, and emotions too powerful to be called "affection" were at work in both of us.

I leaned across the few inches which separated us, and kissed her. I meant it as a message of reassurance and of closeness. But in the next moment we were clinging tightly to one another, swept up in passion and physical need. The abruptness and intensity of those feelings disturbed me, and I pulled myself away from her.

She didn't say anything, but her dark eyes were glowing in that reflective way they sometimes had, and her chest rose and fell in quick, sharp breaths.

"It's been a rough trip," I said, taking deep, deliberate breaths, "and we both need some rest. Sleep well, Tarani."

I saw her thinking about it, wondering whether to press the issue. To my relief, she let it pass. She opened the light, woven blanket and shook it out over herself. As she lay back, she said, in a soft, carefully neutral voice: "Goodnight, Rikardon."

8

I was tired, too. By rights, I should have snuggled into Yoman's bed and slept the night through. Instead, I escaped into the streets of Eddarta.

Here, again, I had a reasonable excuse. I knew little about Eddartan customs, and there's no better way to get information than to buy a few rounds of drinks in a friendly bar. I had planned to go out for a while, anyway, if only to make some discreet inquiries about Gharlas, and his standing among the Lords. I figured to be safe with my own face. It was my sword which identified me to the rogueworld, and Rika was safe with Thymas. In any case, Eddarta's rogueworld was pretty tame—the *organized* thieves lived on the hill.

But the true reason I left was because of Tarani.

In Gandalara, where there was no venereal disease, and birth control was a matter of a woman saying no when her inner awareness warned her she was fertile, intimacy between a consenting couple was considered to be their own business.

If Tarani had been an ordinary Gandalaran woman, I wouldn't have hesitated. If I had just met her, I wouldn't have hesitated.

But I knew Tarani's extraordinary history, and our relationship had an uncertain history of its own.

We had met in Thagorn, when Tarani identified me as the target for a pair of killers traveling with her show. I had felt, and she had later admitted, a sense of recognition in that first meeting. In light of our later adventures, I attributed it to a sort of premonition of our joining forces against Gharlas.

Tarani's involvement in the assassination attempt had come through her association with Molik, the leader of Chizan's rogueworld. At sixteen, still a virgin, she had offered him a deal—her body, and her illusions, in exchange for the capital to create her traveling show.

At eighteen, free of Molik's attentions but not of his memory, she had taken refuge from his unwholesome need of her—a need she felt she had created in Thymas's devotion.

At twenty, only a few weeks ago, she had finally found peace. Given the opportunity to destroy Molik, she had learned that only her guilt tied her to him. When her anger turned to pity, she was truly free.

But that was the *only* thing she had gained, these past few weeks. She had given up the show she had gone through hell to get. She had relinquished the security of her promised marriage to Thymas. She had found her "uncle," only to watch him die, and then discover that he was the father she had never known.

I had seen Tarani regal and strong, the very air around her throbbing with power. I had seen her young and helpless, suffering from my own thoughtless words. She had endured grueling physical demands with the stoic acceptance of a trained soldier. She had survived an emotional crisis that no twenty-year-old girl should be expected to face, and she had come through it sane, hurt but healing. I felt such admiration for her, such tenderness. Her strength of character awed me. Her vulnerability was a warm glow that nestled, trusting, in my thoughts and feelings.

Markasset, with the overriding passion of the young, saw Tarani's response as an indication of her need for emotional comfort. Ricardo, a man still subject to physical need but with a lifetime of wisdom to control it, wanted to give us both time to *understand* the source and destiny of those intense feelings.

I went from bar to bar, pretending to drink a lot of faen. Even while part of my mind was analyzing the information I gleaned from conversation and eavesdropping, I felt my thoughts circling profitlessly around the problem of Tarani.

I weighed responsibility against desire. I tried to decide whether her need was for me, or for anyone—for intimacy, or for assurance that there was more of value in Tarani than her beauty and admitted sexual experience.

In the end, only one thought came to me clearly, as I finished off what would be my final mug of faen:

I'm in love with Tarani. God help us both. I don't want to hurt her.

It was nearly midnight when I returned to Yoman's shop. The door creaked, the stairs groaned. I paused beside Rassa's bedroom door and listened, hoping with one last desperate, pass-the-buck impulse that I hadn't wakened Tarani.

And hoping that I had.

"I'm awake," her voice seemed to answer my thought. I opened the door and stepped into the room. In the dim light, two things stood out. First, she was sitting up, with her back against the wall and the blanket tucked up under her bare arms. Second, her clothes were folded neatly on the ledge beneath the windowsill.

I wasn't aware of any conscious decision. But in less than a second I was across the room, kneeling beside her, taking her in my arms.

Nothing had ever felt so good, not in two lifetimes. She rose to meet me, and the blanket fell aside unheeded. I scrambled out of my tunic, barely aware of her hands helping me. I pulled her close again, holding her carefully, like the treasure she was, and I felt the steady muscles of her dancer's body tremble with eagerness. The touch of her skin on mine made me dizzy with need. Her tongue caressed my tusks as we kissed, sending tendrils of pleasure down my spine.

I felt such joy that I couldn't contain it, couldn't express it. I was transported by the wonder of her body, consenting to be separated from it only for the sake of learning it, by sight and by touch. When I was free of the rest of my clothing, I lay beside her and held her again, wanting to pull her inside my skin, to be entirely and completely one with her.

It was a time of peace, a pause, a lingering. A time of stretched sensitivity, of slow ecstasy. We kissed gently, silent acknowledgment that what we felt for one another was more than bodily need. But the kiss caught fire, and left us breathless and urgent. Tarani lay back, and I rose above her. Her eyes closed in anticipation . . .

"*Oh, Ricardo,*" she whispered.

It was a word Tarani had never heard, couldn't know, would be unable to guess.

The world seemed to freeze around me.

She opened her eyes when she felt the tension thrum through my body. Her hands, caressing my back, grew still.

"What—what did you say, just then?" I panted.

"Say? I only said your name."

"Say it again," I urged.

Doubt flickered in her eyes, and the warm space of air between our bodies seemed to cool. She did what I asked, and said: "Rikardon."

And we both knew it was over.

I drew away from her, and she slid backward to sit up again. She pulled the blanket across her body with a self-consciousness that hurt me like a slap in the face. "It's Molik, isn't it?" she said. Her voice was deadly calm. "You can't bear to be with me because of what I—"

"No!" I nearly shouted the word, appalled that she could put such an interpretation on what had happened. "No, Tarani." More gently.

I took her hand; it lay unresisting, unresponsive, across my fingers.

"Thymas, then?" she said, bitterness creeping in, stinging me.

"Tarani, you have to believe what I'm about to say." She was silent, looking somewhere off to my left. "My . . . failure is in no way your fault. Thymas and Molik have no place in

59

what you and I share. I feel—and you *must* know it, too—that what we wanted tonight *will* happen someday. But not tonight. I'm not sure I understand why, myself. I only know—"

I stopped, lost in misery.

She looked at me then, and I almost wished she would turn away again. The dim light from the window fell across her face. Deep lines etched the smooth skin on her forehead and cheeks.

"I'm frightened, Rikardon," she said, hurriedly, as though she were speaking a dangerous secret.

"Of me?" I asked, surprised and horrified.

"Of whatever is telling you that we cannot . . . that it is not yet time. Of whatever has brought us together, but will not let us *be* together.

"What we are doing, fighting Gharlas, I know it is *right*, Rikardon. But I do not know how it will end. You seem to see things more clearly. Can you tell me that we will *get* the Ra'ira back? That we will both live through what we must do? Can you tell me that there will *be* a 'someday' for us?"

"No, I don't have those answers, Tarani."

Her eyes blazed. "Then *defy* that 'whatever' for once! There may not *be* another chance for us, Rikardon. Give us this moment, at least."

I looked at her. Loving her. Wanting her. And I said: "I can't, Tarani. I'm sorry."

The lines in her face vanished, leaving her skin as pale and smooth as marble. "Please go now," she whispered.

I gathered up my clothes and walked to the door, feeling naked and foolish and miserable, and for the second time in one night, I escaped.

This time my refuge was Yoman's bedroom. When the Gandalaran dawn spread its glowing colors across the cloud-covered sky, I was still sitting and staring, thinking and wondering.

Things that had never made sense fell into place during that watchful night. The mutual recognition Tarani and I

60

had felt, on meeting for the first time. The unusual sophistication of a sixteen-year-old virgin. The abrupt onset of confusion and restlessness that had drawn Tarani from her Recorder training.

The last time I had heard the word Tarani had spoken tonight, I had been Ricardo Carillo, engaged in a harmless and delightful flirtation with Antonia Alderuccio on the deck of a ship, in the middle of the Mediterranean Ocean. The Italian girl had noticed the increasing brightness of a "star", and I had not had time to tell her that I believed it was a meteor. I recall feeling a sense of injustice, as I lost consciousness, that someone as young and beautiful as Antonia had to die so uselessly.

Like me, Antonia had been reborn in Gandalara.

Unlike me, she had been delivered into a host body with a living, vital personality.

I had speculated that, if Markasset had been alive, his familiarity with his body and his surroundings would have given his personality natural control. The period of confusion Tarani had suffered may have been a struggle for control between Tarani and Antonia.

They both won, I thought, watching the early folk moving through the streets of Eddarta. *Tarani is usually in control—and she doesn't seem to have any conscious awareness of Antonia. But grown-up, adult Antonia, accustomed to wealth and wise in the ways of the wealthy, used Tarani's power to handle Molik.*

I remembered Antonia. The way she had laughed. The way she had looked at an old man and seen, not his age, but his experience, the depth and the value of it.

She couldn't have meant the girl harm, I decided. *She was probably only trying to help her get the money she wanted. And she couldn't have been closely integrated into Tarani's personality, or she'd have seen the girl's naiveté, and backed off.*

But there's no doubt she's there, I thought, *and because of her, Tarani's been through the wringer. That horror may be part of whatever is going on here, part of our "destiny."* I slammed my fist on my leg, taking a savage pleasure in the pain it caused. *But it's a hell of a rotten thing to do to a sixteen-year-old girl!*

I heard Tarani stirring in Rassa's room, and I remembered the coldness that had crept over me when I heard Antonia speak through Tarani. It hadn't been fear, or even surprise. How often had I thought that Tarani seemed always to be two different women, one powerful, one helpless?

No, what I had felt in that moment was indecision.

I loved . . . Tarani?

Or Antonia?

9

By the time Tarani had dressed, I had gone out and returned with breakfast. I found her leafing through a series of parchment pages tied at one edge with twine.

"Yoman's ledger," she explained, setting it aside to accept the fruit and bread.

There was a moment of hesitation as her fingers brushed mine, but that was the only sign of what had happened the night before.

Apparently, she's decided on a "business as usual" attitude. Good idea, I approved. *For one thing, we're running short of time.*

"Anything interesting?" I asked.

"He seemed to do a thriving business, even if most of the profit went to Pylomel."

"Pylomel? The *High Lord* is Yoman's landpatron?"

"It surprised me, too," she said. "Why did Yoman not tell us? He knew we wanted information about the High Lord."

"I don't know, but it just adds to the funny feeling I've had all along about Yoman—he was running from something. I feel sure of it."

"Well, it was not poor business, and from the way that fool last night acted, Yoman still has every right to run this shop. But he did not run it alone," she said. "He purchased the fabric and made men's clothes, but Rassa had established herself as a seamstress and designer of women's clothes. I found several commissions for her—from Zefra."

So that's why she's not upset with me this morning, I thought, feeling strangely disappointed. *Finding a way to see her mother is so important that she's forgotten . . .*

You idiot! I scolded myself. *Give the girl what happiness you can, while there's time. And keep your mind on business, OK?*

"Before we go any further with that, Tarani, let me go over what I found out during my drinking tour last night. I think I have a better picture of how Eddarta works, now. Yoman—well, maybe we just didn't know the right questions to ask when we talked to him."

It took me a long time to get back around to Zefra, but Tarani listened patiently, knowing that the more we understood about Eddarta in general, the better our chances of accomplishing *both* things we had come for.

There was no kitchen in Yoman's house, not even shelves where fruit, bread, or Gandalaran liquor, faen or *barut*, could be kept on hand, because Yoman was not a cook or baker. Everyone in Eddarta had a specific trade, and since the Lords took a share of everyone's trade, everyone's trade had to be necessary.

Farmers grew grain, therefore, but could not grind or cook it. Herders sold their glith to slaughterhouses, gave a portion of their profit to the landpatron, then bought table meat from the meat vendor—who passed along a share of *his* profit to *his* landpatron. Tradesmen like Yoman could occasionally benefit directly from their own services—he and Rassa could make their own clothes, for instance—but he had to consider the fabric as wasted inventory.

When the landpatron system had first been mentioned, I had thought of the feudal system of medieval Europe in Ricardo's world. It was a reasonable comparison, since the Lords of Eddarta did own virtually all the land in a huge region in and around the city.

Harthim and six noble families had arrived in Eddarta after their flight from Kä with the greatest, least resistable power—the treasury of the Kingdom. The Eddartans had enjoyed an easy life, with water plentiful and the general level of wealth higher here than anywhere else in Gandalara. The last King had brought an example of an even higher standard of luxury and had taught the Eddartans to crave it, and one by one they had sold their independence for it. When the self-styled Lords had owned Eddarta, they had begun taxing it, winning a hundred-fold return on their initial investments.

The descendents of these seven families lived on in the upper city, called Lord City by the Eddartans. The eldest of each family usually became its Lord. The High Lord, as Gharlas had informed us, was chosen from the descendents of Harthim—his *legitimate* descendents, which left Gharlas hanging loose on the wrong side of the blanket—and was the individual who displayed the strongest mind-power in some sort of test.

I hadn't been able to find an exact date for the building of Lord City, but I suspected that it had been built soon after Harthim's arrival, to protect the Kä refugees from those Eddartans who were discontented with the transition from free enterprise to thinly disguised monopoly. I did learn that each of the seven families had an area of its own inside those massive walls, and that all those areas were linked through what Ricardo would have called a palace. It was a government building called Lord Hall, and it contained meeting rooms, an audience hall, a Council Chamber which had extra-special official significance and, according to the eager gossip of my drinking companions, the hidden entryway to the fabled treasure vault.

"Gharlas is well known here in the lower city," I told Tarani. "Apparently, he's played up his hatred for Pylomel to the point where he's sort of a 'regular guy' to the common folk. Word is that Pylomel isn't fond of him, either, but family rules require that he give Gharlas a place to stay when he's in town."

"Then Gharlas lives in Pylomel's home?"

"If you could call it that. The family areas inside Lord City are huge, with a lot of separate dwellings. Pylomel

65

has probably given Gharlas the cheapest quarters he could manage."

Tarani worried one tusk with her tongue. "Do you remember what Gharlas said about Pylomel's treasure?"

"You mean the secret way he's found into the vault?"

"If we could find the vault, we could reach Gharlas secretly," Tarani said. "Perhaps," she suggested, "if Zefra knows how to enter the vault . . ."

I laughed. Tarani's face darkened, and I touched her arm in apology.

"That's the hard way," I said. "At least, I think it is. Our first step has to be to find Zefra and get the two of you together. We can't do much until we know for sure whether she can—or will—help us against Gharlas."

"She will help if she can," Tarani said.

Take this part easy, I warned myself.

"Tarani, please remember that you don't *know* Zefra yet. The woman who wrote that letter to Volitar lived twenty years ago. This Zefra may not be the same person. For one thing, she's been married to the High Lord all this time."

"You are saying that we should not trust her," Tarani said. "Then why bother to seek her out?"

Her bitterness hurt me. I wanted to put my arms around her, but the scene of the night before told me I had no right to offer her comfort now.

"I believe she *will* want to help us," I said. "But I'm not allowing myself to rely on her help until we know for sure."

That wasn't quite true. The fact of the matter was, everything I had learned about Lord City made me realize that we *needed* some kind of inside help, and I had no idea where else to find it.

"All I'm really saying," I continued, "is that we should be cautious, even with Zefra. We can't tell her the real reason we're here."

She was silent for a few seconds. "I see the wisdom in what you say, Rikardon. I will not speak to Zefra of the Ra'ira. She will help us because Gharlas killed Volitar."

She set down her platter of fruit rinds and picked up the ledger again, the deliberateness of her movements revealing her tension.

"But there is a problem," she added. "These records show appointments in Lord City only at the request of the buyer."

"Something else I learned last night—there's going to be some kind of fancy ceremony in a few days, and Lord City is really stirred up about it. Do you see a recent commission from Zefra?"

She examined the book. "No. There was an appointment scheduled two seven-days ago, but there is no notation of it having been kept. Yoman and Rassa must have left before then." She looked up at me and smiled. "You are thinking that the High Lord's wife should have a new dress for this occasion?" I nodded. "But *she* will have to send for Rassa. How will she know—?"

"I'll tell her," I said. "It seems that each Lord has his own private guard. Whether that's traditional, or a defense against assassination by the next in line or another Lord, I don't know. But I should be able to get inside Lord City to talk to somebody about hiring on."

Her head tilted to one side. "That would leave you the entire city to search. Could Yoman and Rassa not simply present themselves at the gate with—say, a *gift* for Zefra or Pylomel?" Tarani suggested.

"They might. Do we *have* such a gift, or could you make one in less than a day?"

She shook her head.

"No, I didn't think so, and if my calculations are right, Gharlas will be here tomorrow or the next day. It's important that we get inside that city before he arrives.

"I'm going up this morning to try to get a job as one of Pylomel's mercenaries. That will get me into the right area. I'll just have to bet on having a chance to talk to Zefra, and I'll ask her to send for you."

"I could come with you, Rikardon. If I projected the image of a man—"

"You need to conserve your strength, Tarani." I remembered how she had looked just after we arrived in Yoman's shop—washed-out, haggard.

She remembered, too. She nodded, reluctantly. "What if the guards are watching for you?" she asked.

"They won't be. That's one thing I'm pretty sure of. Gharlas has no army of his own, and Pylomel wouldn't do him any favors."

I hoped I was right. As I stood up I felt the surge of tension and alertness that made Markasset the excellent fighter he was.

"The sooner we get free of Yoman and Rassa, the better I'll like it," I said. "I'll go up to the gate. You just sit tight, and don't open the shop. If customers come by, make the excuse that you've just returned from a long journey, and Yoman is still recuperating. Promise them you'll be open tomorrow. If we aren't both inside Lord City by tomorrow, we may have to take up tailoring for a living."

She stared at me, then smiled a little, and finally chuckled, shaking her head. "There is surely no other like you in Gandalara," she said. "This seems less a plan than merely the start of one—but it does seem to be our only choice. I will spend the day selecting fabric samples to take with me when I receive Zefra's summons."

"The one major hitch to this plan," I said, "is that I may have to *take* that guard job, and I might get stuck inside the city. If I *don't* return tonight, and you don't hear from Zefra tomorrow, don't panic. Just sit tight, play Rassa, and cover for Yoman. If you haven't heard from me or Zefra by the time Thymas gets here, make whatever plans seem right. You'll have to find another way to get inside, but I'll be watching for you, and trying to get a line on Gharlas."

She stood up, and for a second or two I thought—hoped—she would cross the few paces between us and let me hold her once more before we went our separate ways. But if that had been her impulse, she controlled it by stepping backward and hugging the ledger to her chest.

"Be cautious at every step, Rikardon," she said. "Eddarta is an unhappy place, and full of treachery. I feel it."

"Thank you for the warning," I said.

"I give it for my own sake," she said. "You ... are important to me."

A foolish happiness washed over me. I had thought I'd destroyed whatever feelings Tarani was beginning to have for me. But those few simple words, spoken from all the way across the room, were a promise of another chance.

"As you are, to me," I said, and left the room.

I nearly ran down the stairs and out into the street. Then I paused to take a few deep breaths, and began to walk toward the boulevard that would take me up the hill to Lord City.

10

It's a little-known fact of life that, now and then, the odds *have* to turn in your favor. It might have been the warm feeling I carried away from Tarani, or it might have been the adrenaline surge of finally, after all this time, reaching the point of action—but I felt good about that short-notice plan as I climbed the zigzag avenue toward Lord City. I had a feeling things were going to work out right, for a change.

It was still pretty early in the day, and I walked up with a column of burdened wagons, dragged along by unhappy vleks. I looked back once or twice and was impressed, again, by the advantage the walled city would have in battle. This place had been built by frightened men hundreds of generations ago, and they had legalized and bequeathed their paranoia to its present occupants.

It seemed odd that any such unbalanced system could have survived for so long, but Gandalara was a world that changed slowly. Innovations had been made—the Gandalarans had a remarkably efficient economy and a respectable technology, hampered as they were by their lack of elemental iron. But they had an extra weight entrenching the natural conservatism of people who always feel the tentative balance of their survival. The All-Mind.

It wasn't just the "older generation" who set up the rules in Gandalara. It was the memory and experience of all previous generations—and that was a tough opponent to beat down. Gandalarans had struck a compromise between the need for change and the need for stability. Trades were family property, passed along from one generation to the next, so that improvements in irrigation techniques or the sand/ash mixture for glass were preserved each step of the way. Eddarta was the first place I had been in which each person was so strictly limited to his own trade; it reduced prideful occupations to the status of assembly-line construction.

Eddarta had another unique quality—the people of Eddarta used their river for transport of cargo and only cargo. There wasn't even a Gandalaran word to imply a *person* floating on water. Tarani and I had seen miles and miles of thick rope stretched along the riverbanks on our way toward the city. Vleks were tied to that line, and small, shallow-draft barges were tied to the vleks and hauled along. There was usually one person on the riverbank with a rear guiderope, and sometimes two or three other people with poles to keep the barge from beaching itself in the reedy growth along the banks.

The traveled areas of the river had their banks trimmed of the whitish reeds that grew taller than men, and the reed harvest served the secondary function of providing building material for the rafts. Bundles of reeds were cut, then bound tightly together. The open ends of the reeds were sealed somehow to create a long, floating log. Several logs, lashed together, made a raft.

We had seen such rafts hauling stuff upstream and controlling speed downstream—only on the smoothest, slowest stretches of water. A few yards of rapids called for wagon transport beside the river until the current calmed down again.

A series of those rafts operated on the branch of the Tashal which flowed through Lord City. I saw two stone archways as I approached the high walls. One admitted only people; the other admitted cargo. The wagons which had toiled up the slope were unloaded onto rafts, and the goods were taken inside by Lord City boatmen, who were dealing with faster current, here, than I had seen out in the country—the cataracts above and below the city kept the water moving pretty fast. To counteract the speed of the current, the Lord City boatmen had contrived a pretty complicated two-bank system.

One vlek team did the primary work of hauling, while the team on the opposite bank kept the raft aligned properly. Both banks had two levels of pathways, so that while one set of vleks hauled a raft upstream on the higher paths, another set provided brakes for a raft going downstream. The downstream rafts were pulled toward the opposite bank, and the ropes were given plenty of slack. It looked to be a pretty tricky proposition, keeping the upstream raft from fouling itself on the downstream ropes— but I watched the operation go smoothly a couple of times.

"You got business here?" A voice at my elbow called me away from watching the river. I turned around to face a huge man with leather straps crisscrossing his bare chest. Bronze discs studded the leather. He was wearing desert-style trousers instead of a leather breechclout, but his muscles and stance and attitude reminded Ricardo of a badly researched movie about Roman gladiators.

I put a smile on my face. "I hope so," I said. "I'm just in from Chizan. A fellow I met in a bar last night said the High Lord might be in need of another sword. I could use the job."

The man looked me up and down. He was a brawny type, with very prominent supraorbital ridges, a low-slung jaw, and hair on his knuckles.

"Experience?" he snapped.

"Four years as a caravan guard, saw some action with the Sharith before the master gave in and paid the toll."

The guard snorted. "Them turncoats."

The subjects adopt the masters' politics, I thought. *The original Eddartans had no reason to hate the Sharith.*

Or did they? After all, the Sharith more or less drove Harthim into settling here, which hasn't done them much good.

Hey, pay attention! I ordered myself. *Is he giving you advice?*

That's exactly what he was doing. I reached back into my short-term memory and recovered the words I had missed. "All the Lords are hiring," he had said. He went on: "But the High Guard has the best pay and—" He smirked. On that face, it wasn't a pretty sight. "—and the best extra benefits."

"Sounds great," I said. "What's the catch?"

The big man roared out a laugh, then slapped me on the back so hard that I staggered away from him. "You're a wise one, you are. You gotta pass a test to land a job on the High Guard."

"What kind of test?" I asked, bracing myself for a fight.

He saw me tense up, and laughed again. "You got the right idea, friend, but the wrong man." He pointed to his chest with his thumb. "I'm Sendar. The man you need to see is Obilin. And I'll give you this much warning—don't judge him by his size. Or," he added, sobering up, "by his smile."

"Well, I'm grateful for your advice, Sendar," I said. "I'm Lakad." It was an alias I had used so often that it felt natural now. "Where will I find Obilin?"

Sendar took my sword—it was the first time I'd been really glad that I'd left Rika behind—and said I could pick it up on my way out, if I wouldn't be staying. He gave me explicit directions on how to find Pylomel's guardhouse, and warned me to announce my presence quickly.

Here was the luck I had felt was waiting for me as I climbed the hill. It just so happened that Pylomel's guardhouse was located close to the High Lord's garden, a favorite place for the lady of the house to walk, of a morning. Sendar warned me that sneaking around the garden was an easy way to get killed.

I thanked him again.

"One more thing," he added. "I've got gate duty all day. I'll expect to see you come back through here, or to find you in the barracks tonight. If you're not one place or the other, I'll know you lied to me. And anybody who lies to me don't live long."

"A-huh," I said. "Well, see you later, Sendar." I didn't

feel the confidence I was trying to project, but I fooled the guard. He laughed and slapped me on my way.

I had wondered why the complicated river transport was necessary. I discovered the reason as I stepped through the stone archway and into Lord City. Except for the river animals, vleks weren't permitted inside the walls. The cargo was unloaded and delivered by an endless chain of slaves. Not *servants*, who could be categorized as people who practiced their trades—cooking, cleaning—in the exclusive employ of one individual or household. These were *slaves*—thin, dejected creatures whose only value seemed to be that they were cleaner and quieter and more cooperative than vleks.

I had known that slaves were used in Eddarta, particularly in the copper mines and the bronze foundries. Theoretically, they were criminals who were sentenced to a period of service. But Dharak had talked about *selling* slaves to the Eddartans as if it were a routine thing, so I assumed that there were less "official" ways of obtaining the muscle needed to mine copper.

I had felt a distant sort of sympathy for Eddarta's slaves, but I wasn't prepared for the shock of actually seeing such people. Somehow it seemed more deplorable for the Eddartans to use slaves for immediate, private service than to employ them for broad economic gain in the copper mines. In the shock of seeing slavery close up, I realized how unfair that distinction was. *Any* use of men and women as slaves was totally undefendable.

I didn't dare let my outrage show, so I turned my face away and aimed my steps in the direction of the large central building. It stood some five hundred yards away from the water, and looked to be two stories or more. It was octagonal, with one face opening on the stone-paved avenue which led through the entryway, and one face fronting each of the seven walkways.

Columns composed of shallow marble blocks, carved to stack smoothly, supported canvas awnings stretched across wooden frames. The awnings shaded the area around Lord Hall, giving an effect much like the columned porticoes of

Ricardo's ancient Rome, and extended to provide shade for the seven walkways which radiated from Lord Hall, each one joining the entrances to the Hall with the entrances to one of the seven family areas.

Sendar had said that Pylomel's living area was the largest in the city, and was located to my right. The walkway which joined it to Lord Hall led across a pontoon bridge; a channel had been diverted from the river itself to run through Pylomel's much-prized garden.

There was no denying that Lord City was beautiful. The segments of territory between the radiating walkways had been landscaped with meticulous care, and these mini-gardens boasted a variety of trees and bushes, as well as flowering plants I hadn't seen anywhere else. The overall impression was one of lushness and wealth—undoubtedly the object of the careful arrangements.

The lovely garden areas proved an obstacle to me, however, for they implied that it was mandatory for visitors to keep their feet on the pavement. Even though I was standing nearer to the entrance of Pylomel's area than to Lord Hall, I had to follow the avenue up to the immense building, then turn back toward the river along the walkway.

Sendar had said, and it was readily confirmed, that the entrance to every family area led into the courtyard bounded on either side by wings of the guardhouse. As I walked carefully across the pontoon bridge, I could see two men on duty at the arched stone entrance to Pylomel's area. The courtyard was visible through the archway. Beyond it, a pathway branched immediately. From what Sendar had told me, I assumed that the left-hand branch led into the garden, and the right one led around to the front entrance of the huge building that had to be Pylomel's home.

The luck I was feeling was still with me. The attention of the outer guard was directed to the unloading platform. The weight of one raft's load had been poorly distributed, the men unloading it hadn't noticed until too late, and it looked as though load and workmen all were going for a swim very shortly.

I stepped into the shrubbery and moved quietly to my left. A low stone wall running from the guardhouse back to the river was a token marking of the boundary of Pylomel's personal domain; high brush just inside that wall provided privacy for his garden. I heard a step, and crouched behind a bush just in time to avoid being seen by a guard patrolling that short stretch of wall.

Just then, a sound I had attributed to the river came clear—another guard at the water's edge, drinking. I crouched back out of sight as he walked into view. He stood beside the wall, midway from the guardhouse to the river.

Two guards, one stationary, one patrolling, I thought, and spent a few seconds swearing under my breath.

There's no way to get into that garden without taking out one of those guards, which would kill my little play-act about wanting work.

I sat tight and thought about it for a while. I could try for the guard job, and hope to have the opportunity to contact Zefra later. I could turn around and leave right now, and tell Sendar I'd changed my mind about the job, once I saw Obilin. But both courses would result in delays we *couldn't* afford.

Something made me decide to chance it—a whiff of fragrance that was subtly nonfloral. Perfume.

The use of perfume was rare in Gandalara, but it seemed to be, socially, the exclusive property of wealthy women. I *knew*, so surely that I'd have bet my tusks, that I had come at the right time. Zefra was walking in Pylomel's garden.

I summoned all the patience I could, and waited my chance to move. Little by little, while the guard's attention was fixed somewhere, I crept closer to the wall, keeping to the cover of the larger bushes. I had my big chance when I heard the hollering and splashing from the river as the poorly balanced load finally knocked a couple of the workers into the river. Both guards moved toward the guardhouse to get a clearer view of what was going on.

I ran for the wall, slid over it, and made my way on my belly, slowly, through the tangled growth at the base of the privacy hedge.

The garden was truly beautiful. The channel which brought the river water formed a series of tiny streams and ponds, and every kind of plant Markasset had ever seen—plus a few species that were new to him—was represented in the garden. But I didn't have the time, or the inclination, to admire the botanical genius of Pylomel's gardener.

Zefra was there.

11

She wasn't alone. There were guards *inside* the garden, and though they stood at a respectful distance, I got the distinct impression that they weren't so much protecting Zefra as keeping her under surveillance.

She was walking along the pathways slowly, bending to examine flowers, meandering in my direction. I eased myself to my feet, but stayed hidden in the hedge, waiting. If she kept on going, she would walk right by me . . .

She stopped to examine a flower on the bush next to me. I was stunned by her close resemblance to Tarani. Her body carried a few extra pounds for her twenty extra years, but the fine shape of her face, the lustrous black of her headfur, even the graceful way she used her hands—I could see Tarani clearly within the frame of her mother.

I hope she has Tarani's coolness, too, I thought. *I don't have time to do this gently.*

"Volitar is dead," I whispered. Her hand, cupping the flower, tightened to crush it. "Tarani is in Eddarta. Send for Rassa, the dressmaker. Your daughter will come to you instead."

"*She must not be seen in this place,*" Zefra whispered fiercely.

"She will be seen only as Rassa," I said.

The woman gasped, and her composure almost deserted her. To cover her sudden motion, she moved past me and began to examine a different flower.

"Then Tarani has learned to use her mind-gift," she

said. "Who are you, and why have you brought Tarani into danger?"

I refrained from asking her why she assumed that *I* had done the bringing. Instead, I answered: "I'm a friend, Zefra. Tarani and I have an important job to do. We need your help. She'll explain when she sees you."

"And if I refuse?" she asked. But her eyes were closed, and her hands were trembling. I didn't say anything, and after a moment, she sighed deeply. "I will do it. Tell me your name."

"Rikardon."

"If my daughter suffers harm from this, Rikardon, I will not rest until your heart has been fed to Pylomel's dralda."

She cried out suddenly, and put her finger to her lips as though a thorn had stuck her. She turned and hurried out of the garden, and the guards watched her go.

So they didn't see me slide back across the wall.

The outside guard was returning from the ruckus at the river. He was, in fact, less than ten feet away from me. He was saying something over his shoulder to another guard, so that his head was turned.

There was nowhere I could go in a hurry, so I stood up and walked toward him. "Excuse me?"

He jumped. When he landed again, his sword was in his hand.

This guy's no slouch, I thought. *And Sendar—I wouldn't care to take him on. Pylomel's got some good-quality heavies on his side.*

"Where in the name of Harthim did you come from?" he asked, looking around. The wall into the garden was the closest concealment; I saw his eyes narrow with suspicion.

"Are you Obilin?" I asked him, to distract his attention from the garden. It worked. He looked at me as though I should be stepped on.

"No," he grunted. "Who are you?"

"Name's Lakad," I said. "Fellow named Sendar, at the gate, said I should talk to Obilin about joining the High Lord's guard."

"He must have given you directions, too," the man said. "You're pretty far from the main path."

"Yeah, he warned me about that," I said. I tried to grin companionably, but I'm sure the effect wasn't very convincing. "I just got sidetracked by these trees—I've never seen any like this."

Half-true, I thought.

"They're pretty rare, all right," the man said, straightening his shoulders and puffing out his chest as if he personally had planted every one of those trees.

"But listen," he added gruffly, "don't wander around until you've signed up—otherwise you won't live to meet Obilin."

"If you'll tell me where he is, I'll go straight over there now," I said sincerely.

"I'll show you," he said, grabbing my arm and dragging me toward the walkway and the entrance to the guardhouse. I dug in my heels; he stopped and looked at me in surprise.

Not used to folks who don't jump when you say so? I wondered. *Well, I'm not going to start my career as a fifth columnist by being pushed around.*

"I can walk very well alone, thanks," I said, and pulled my arm out of his grasp. There was a visible pulse at his temple as he considered contesting the point, then he shrugged and waved me ahead of him.

Up to this point, I'd had some choices left. I could have gone back out the gate, sent Tarani in to see her mother alone, and made further plans after their meeting. *If* Tarani weren't spotted. *If* Tarani didn't just decide to stay with the mother she had never met before. *If* one of the hundred other possible complications that would keep me chewing my nails didn't actually happen.

Unappealing as it was, the choice had been feasible up to the time I was buttonholed next to the forbidden garden. As I walked through the brick-faced archway and turned left into the common room of the guardhouse, I knew I was committed to our plan, sketchy as it was. The next step was to get myself hired on, which would involve, if I had understood Sendar correctly, a competitive test of my fighting skills. In other words (in *Ricardo's* words), a brawl.

The stone walls of the rectangular room were topped by a high, flat ceiling made of unfinished wood. There were several long tables and benches, and padded stone shelves around the edges of the room which seemed to serve as lounging seats. A game of *mondea* was in progress at one table—it had the same persistence among Gandalara's military-style folk that poker had in Ricardo's world.

"Watch him," my escort growled to the players, then left by a door which led off to the right, and which he closed behind him.

The four players looked up at me briefly. Appearances aren't everything, I know. But from the look of those scarred, slack-jawed faces, I'd have bet there wasn't an ounce of charm among them.

I smiled. "I'm not going anywhere," I said. "And I'd rather watch you. Who's winning?"

"Me," growled the biggest man, who was missing one ear and several teeth. "You can watch. Quietly."

I nodded, and moved closer. It was a fast game, with rules that were slightly different from those I had learned from Bareff and Liden during my short stay with the Sharith. I became so completely absorbed in the action of the *mondeana*, the dicelike playing pieces, that I was surprised by a light touch on my shoulder.

I turned around to face a very small man, while the clatter and hooting at and around the dice table crashed into absolute silence.

"I'm Obilin," the little man said. Then he hit me in the stomach.

It was a sharp, high-powered jab of surprising power. He delivered it with his left hand, and I saw his right get ready to swing at my head as I doubled over. I let my knees fold, so that I dropped clear to the floor, moving faster than he expected. Then I swung my body to my left, catching Obilin's midriff on my shoulder, and heaved myself upright again, sending the little man flying into the air. While I took short, quick breaths to try to get back my wind, I watched Obilin right himself in the air and come down on his feet.

Chairs scraped away from the table behind me, and I heard the clinking as the coins and mondeana were gathered up hastily.

"Wouldn't you rather do this outside?" I suggested. "Not much room to move around in here."

The smile was still there, and I heard a soft, whispery laugh that made my skin crawl.

"Good," he said. "No questions. No complaints. Immediate grasp of the situation. Very good, Lakad.

"But, to answer your question, no, we'll stay here. A fighter has to be aware of his surroundings, as well as his opponent, don't you agree?"

One minute he was standing quite still, nearly ten feet away from me. Suddenly he was on top of the table next to me, a kick heading for my chin.

I ducked aside, grabbed for the moving leg, missed it, grabbed for his balance leg, but it was already gone. He was on the floor on the other side of the table, bouncing.

You certainly are a fast mother, Obilin, I thought at him, as I hit the floor to dodge his two-fisted dive across the table. *And smooth,* I added, as I watched him somersault down the narrow aisle between tables and come up on his feet, facing me. *How can you judge distances so well?*

The answer occurred to me almost immediately.

Because you're not distracted by defending yourself, that's how. You stage these fights in here to keep your opponent a safe distance away from you. Your game is all offense, Obilin, I realized. *Let's see what happens when you're cornered.*

The other men in the room were reclining on the benches against the walls. If I'd had time, I would have been surprised that they weren't calling bets back and forth, or encouraging one of us. But they were quiet, and I noticed that only long enough to be glad for the chance to give my complete attention to Obilin.

He came at me again, aiming his right arm and using the inertia of his self-propelled body to add weight to the intended blow. I stepped aside with the intention of snagging him and pinning him down—but he had anticipated me. His right hand missed me, but his left hand came up out of nowhere and slammed the side of my head, and sent me reeling. I let myself go loose, and I groped for support from a nearby table, lowering myself to the bench. Obilin closed in, the smile unchanged on his face, his short stature towering over me where I sat. Then he made his first mistake.

He grabbed my head with both hands, to steady it as a target for his knee. I let him begin the knee jab, but then I snapped my head up, grabbed that uppraised leg, and yanked with all my strength. Obilin was *very* quick; I felt his body register the danger the moment I touched his leg, and he tried to brace himself to resist. But that hard pull brought him down, with his legs scissored around the bench. I had time to deliver one sharp, backhanded blow before he slipped away from me, rolled, and stood up.

The smile still looked the same. It still scared me.

"Well done, Lakad," he said. "You impress me. Still, the true test of a fighter is in his sword work, wouldn't you say?" He held out his hand, and someone slid a sword, hilt-first, across the nearest table to me. I left it there.

"Well, Lakad?" he said, gesturing at the sword.

Suddenly, I wanted to laugh. *Didn't I watch this scene in a pirate movie with Burt Lancaster?* I wondered, a little hysterically. Then I looked at Obilin's face, and a new thought chilled me. That smile was genuine, and reflected real pleasure, real anticipation.

I stopped being scared, and started to dislike Obilin. A lot.

I picked up the sword, just in time to block his first blow. He was fast, but not really strong. As long as I could anticipate him, and get a block up in time, he couldn't touch me. But the very speed of his attack kept me backing away, and on the defensive.

Same game plan, I realized. *All offense.* I realized

something else, looking into the small man's grinning face. *The way to get hired on around here isn't to beat this guy. If I win, he'll hate me. On the other hand, if I lose badly, he'll have no reason to hire me. I need to show some capability, and then lose. And somehow, in the process, stay alive.*

That last seemed to be the hardest part, because there was no doubt that Obilin was sincerely trying to kill me. If I *gave* him an opening . . .

I had backed up against a table, and suddenly the chance I needed was there. He brought in a low slash and, instead of blocking it, I jumped the blade and scrambled up on the table. On my knees, I had the advantage of extra striking room in a downward swing, and for an instant, Obilin was defending himself against the overhead attack.

Then he did what I expected; he grabbed a leg of the table and heaved, to knock me off balance. I fell off, banging my shoulder on the stone-paved floor, and when I stopped rolling, I felt a sword point against my throat.

The smile was still there. "You're hired," he said, and put away his sword.

12

I spent the next couple of hours getting acquainted with the area and with the rules, courtesy of a wrinkled old man who seemed to be a butler-type person for the barracks. He issued me a sword—to be used until Sendar came off duty and returned my own (Thymas's)—and delivered all his information in a bored monotone, eyes and voice aimed into the air above my left shoulder.

My quarters were surprisingly comfortable—one large room, divided into sleeping and visiting areas. The duty roster was complicated, but not hard to live with. A series of shifts (six hours on, six off) for three days, then one full day off. Meals were served in a community room, except on your day off. Then, if you requested it, a woman would serve your dinner in your rooms, and stay with you through the night.

So that's what Sendar meant by the "extra benefits" to be had by working for Pylomel.

"The High Lord is very generous," I said to the old man, whose name was Willon. "Who do I ask for this extra service?"

"The High Lord ain't got much to do with it," Willon said, looking straight at me, finally. "You ask *me* when you're ready."

"Ah-huh. And how much do I pay *you?*" I asked.

"Not a zak," he said. I must have let my skepticism show, because he got defensive. "Oh, I get paid, all right—a portion of what they get. And *before you ask,* you don't pay them, either. The Guard has a friend who really appreciates the work we do."

Suddenly, it all made sense. "Would this friend's name be Gharlas?"

The old man peered at me suspiciously. "How'd you know that?"

I shrugged. "I may have just come into town, Willon, but I know how to keep my ears open. And, *before you ask*, my mouth is shut."

"Good," he said, with an emphatic nod, and the matter was closed. "You'll be on the supper shift this evening, so you best take a short rest."

I did, in fact, lie down on the fluffy pallet for a few minutes. But I was too restless to sleep.

So far, I had been able to control the execution of our plan, at least to some extent. I had been very lucky, too—I was well aware of that. But I had been the one taking action, and I had felt a sense of confidence, knowing that success or failure were, for the moment, entirely my responsibility.

Now it was different. The next step was Tarani's play. I felt a different kind of confidence in her, a sureness that she would do whatever was necessary. But not being able to *see* what she did was like an unreachable itch.

Finally, I went into the common room. I watched the mondea game for a little while, sat in for a few rounds. But I kept feeling more and more restless, and finally had to excuse myself and walk around. I found myself in the court between the barracks and the "back door" of Pylomel's home.

Tarani/Rassa was coming through the entryway, followed by two slaves who were loaded down with bolts of cloth. She gave me a strained smile, and I grinned back in relief. She was totally unsurprised to find me waiting for her.

So that's what a mild compulsion feels like! I thought. *That paralysis Gharlas laid on us in Dyskornis must have been something different—a blocking, rather than a forcing. But he was able to compel Thymas*, I remembered, and shivered in sympathy for what the boy must have suffered. *I'm glad that kind of power scares Tarani.*

I felt another mental nudge, and moved out into the courtyard so that my path intersected Tarani's. Her hand caught my arm, and I fell into step beside her while I watched a shadowy, semitransparent version of myself move past and out of the way. I pulled my arm through her fingers until I could hold her hand, and I squeezed it, hoping the pressure would give her some reassurance.

She was trembling, but I was at a loss to guess whether it was the strain of the illusion—two illusions, now that I was "invisible"—apprehension about the situation, or anticipation of meeting her mother. I kept close to her, exactly beside her, hoping that I was minimizing the effort she needed to keep the illusions intact.

Instead of following the well-marked pathway which led to the front door of the huge house, Tarani and I followed an extension of the courtyard to a small door in the back of the building—the servant or merchant entrance. As we approached the doorway, the guard stepped aside to let a small man come out into the court. I had no difficulty recognizing Obilin. He grinned widely when he saw Rassa, and deliberately took a stance which blocked the entry.

"So you've made the wise choice, after all, Rassa?"

Tarani stopped, and her hand tightened in mine.

"The only choice I have made is to obey the summons of Zefra, who has asked me to design a gown for her for the Celebration Dance. Please, let me pass by."

"Why, of course, dear dressmaker," he said, stepping to our right and waving the entourage through with an elaborate bow. But his grin never faded, and as Tarani passed him, one lightning-quick hand closed on her arm. He leaned close to her and whispered: "But you don't think, for a minute, that you will leave here again before the High Lord gets what he wants, do you?"

"My concern now is what the lady Zefra wants. Release me."

He did, and it was a good thing. There have been few times in my life when I wanted so badly to hit somebody.

But I realized, as Tarani and I walked carefully through the doorway into the High Lord's home, that it wasn't Obilin I wanted to hit.

I finally pinned down the source of the uneasiness that had plagued me since Tarani and I had assumed the identities of Rassa and Yoman. I had had the feeling that both of them had been running away from something specific. Now it seemed so simple that I wondered why I hadn't figured it out before now.

The talk I had heard last night had been full of complaints against the High Lord's habit of appropriating any woman among his landservants who caught his fancy. It was only a now-and-then sort of thing, apparently, or resistance to it would have been more cohesive. But the women never returned to their homes.

Rassa had met with Zefra frequently, so that Pylomel would have had many opportunities to see her and be attracted by her unusual beauty. There had been some warning of his interest, and Yoman had made the choice to leave his entire life behind, in order to save his daughter from that fate. Yoman didn't tell us that Pylomel was his landpatron—perhaps he feared we would guess the situation and back out on the plan which promised him and his daughter a better chance of escape.

So Yoman had sacrificed two strangers for his daughter's safety. Try as I might, though, I couldn't blame him. The face I *really* wanted to smash was Pylomel's.

Inside the entryway, Tarani pulled me aside and gestured to the two slaves to go ahead of us. They went, walking with a quiet acceptance of their burdens which seemed less stoic than merely resigned. Tarani sighed softly as we started to follow them. I looked at her, and I put my arm around her for support while we walked through a labyrinth of hallways.

I feel like a white rat, I thought, hopelessly trying to keep track of the twists and turns in the route we covered. It seemed as though every High Lord since Harthim had added his own shape and taste to the building. I had a vague sense of remaining near the garden side of the

Introducing the first and only complete hardcover collection of Agatha Christie's mysteries

Now you can enjoy the
greatest mysteries ever written
in a magnificent
Home Library Edition.

Discover Agatha Christie's world of mystery, adventure and intrigue

Agatha Christie's timeless tales of mystery and suspense offer something for every reader—mystery fan or not—young and old alike. And now, you can build a complete hardcover library of her world-famous mysteries by subscribing to The Agatha Christie Mystery Collection.

This exciting Collection is your passport to a world where mystery reigns supreme. Volume after volume, you and your family will enjoy mystery reading at its very best.

You'll meet Agatha Christie's world-famous detectives like Hercule Poirot, Jane Marple, and the likeable Tommy and Tuppence Beresford.

In your readings, you'll visit Egypt, Paris, England and other exciting destinations where murder is always on the itinerary. And wherever you travel, you'll become deeply involved in some of the most ingenious and diabolical plots ever invented ... "cliff-hangers" that only Dame Agatha could create!

It all adds up to mystery reading that's so good ... it's almost criminal. And it's yours every month with The Agatha Christie Mystery Collection.

Solve the greatest mysteries of all time. The Collection contains all of Agatha Christie's classic works including *Murder on the Orient Express, Death on the Nile, And Then There Were None, The ABC Murders* and her ever-popular whodunit, *The Murder of Roger Ackroyd*.

Each handsome hardcover volume is Smythe sewn and printed on high quality acid-free paper so it can withstand even the most murderous treatment. Bound in Sussex-blue simulated leather with gold titling, The Agatha Christie Mystery Collection will make a tasteful addition to your living room, or den.

Ride the Orient Express for 10 days without obligation.
To introduce you to the Collection, we're inviting you to examine the classic mystery, *Murder on the Orient Express*, without risk or obligation. If you're not completely satisfied, just return it within 10 days and owe nothing.

However, if you're like the millions of other readers who love Agatha Christie's thrilling tales of mystery and suspense, keep *Murder on the Orient Express* and pay just $9.95 plus postage and handling.

You will then automatically receive future volumes once a month as they are published on a fully returnable, 10-day free-examination basis. No minimum purchase is required, and you may cancel your subscription at any time.

This unique collection is not sold in stores. It's available only through this special offer. So don't miss out, begin your subscription now. Just mail this card today.

☐ Yes! Please send me *Murder on the Orient Express* for a 10-day free-examination and enter my subscription to <u>The Agatha Christie Mystery Collection</u>. If I keep *Murder on the Orient Express*, I will pay just $9.95 plus postage and handling and receive one additional volume each month on a fully returnable 10-day free-examination basis. There is no minimum number of volumes to buy, and I may cancel my subscription at any time.   07013

☐ I prefer the deluxe edition bound in genuine leather for $24.95 per volume plus shipping and handling, with the same 10-day free-examination.   07054

Name_____

Address_____

City_____ State_____ Zip_____

AC12

**Send No Money...
But Act Today!**

BUSINESS REPLY CARD

FIRST CLASS   PERMIT NO. 2154   HICKSVILLE, N.Y.

Postage will be paid by addressee:

The Agatha Christie
Mystery Collection
Bantam Books
P.O. Box 956
Hicksville, N.Y. 11802

house, and I was sure that we were on the second floor, but I also knew it would be hopeless to find our way out again without help.

I hope Zefra is on our side, I thought.

Finally, the slaves slowed and stopped. Tarani straightened up, and only our hands touched as we passed the slaves to stand in front of a large double door. There was a guard on either side of the door; I felt naked and exposed, and I thought: *If Tarani's illusions can hide me when I'm face-to-face with these guys, they can do anything*.

A young girl answered Tarani's knock.

"I am Rassa," Tarani told her. "I am to create a gown for the lady Zefra."

"She awaits you," the girl said in a shy but formal voice, and opened both doors to admit "Rassa" and the goods-bearing slaves. I entered beside her; Tarani's hand was clutching mine so hard that I worried about something breaking.

We were in a small, rectangular sitting room that had doors in both narrow walls. A stone ledge ran along the bottom of one long wall, and was padded with embroidered cushions that matched those in the three free-standing chairs. A ledge along the other doorless wall was left bare, and it was there that the slaves placed the bolts of cloth under Tarani's direction. When the cloth was properly displayed, and the slaves had left, the girl spoke again.

"The lady Zefra asked me to bring you her greetings, Rassa. She will be with you shortly. In the meantime, I have another errand to perform. With your permission..."

The girl bowed and left through the entry door. Tarani sighed and relaxed as the illusions vanished; I caught her and lowered her into one of the chairs. No sooner was she seated, however, than the inner door opened and Zefra came in. Clearly, she had been waiting for the slave-girl to leave us alone.

Tarani looked around toward the door as she heard it open, and she stared for a long time while Zefra stood, as if turned to stone, and stared back. I was kneeling beside Tarani, but I might as well have been still invisible. I must have responded subconsciously to their exclusion of me, for by the time Zefra moved, I was on the other side of the room, pressing my back against the double door.

Tarani was still shaky from the strain of holding the illusions so long, but she stood up as Zefra approached her. The older woman's hands reached out to frame the girl's face for another long, searching look, and then Zefra moved closer and placed her cheek against Tarani's. Suddenly they were holding one another, gasping softly and rocking back and forth.

Right smack in the middle of it, someone knocked on the door behind me, so heavily that the vibrations sent me staggering toward the women. A voice boomed through the closed doors: "OPEN FOR THE HIGH LORD."

I ran for the inner doors, grabbing Tarani's hand as I passed. "He wants Rassa," I whispered, dragging Tarani toward the door.

Zefra caught the girl's hand and hauled the other way, stopping me. "Then he must find her here," she said. "I know you're weary, daughter," she whispered, touching Tarani's face again, "but you must keep Rassa's illusion a bit longer."

"Rikardon—" Tarani started to say.

"He *can* hide in my apartment," Zefra said. "You need only keep Rassa's illusion. *Can you do it?*"

Tarani nodded.

"You—" she said to me. "Go through the door. Tarani will be safe—you must trust me."

"OPEN FOR THE HIGH LORD!" the voice boomed again. I dived through the open door and pulled it nearly shut behind me. Then I drew my sword and waited with my ear to the door. I trusted Zefra because the woman I had met matched the woman I had imagined from her letter. But Pylomel was an unknown quantity.

I heard some quick movements in the room, then Zefra opened the door. "Why did you not open on the first summons, wife?" said a voice I disliked instantly. It was whiny and carried a sarcastic, affected petulance.

"Your pardon, Pylomel," Zefra said coolly, "but I was

disrobed. My dressmaker is here, as you see. She was measuring me for a new gown for the Celebration Dance."

"And would it be so inappropriate for a husband to see his wife disrobed?" said the nasty voice again.

"Not at all. But would my husband like his announcer to see me in such a state?"

I heard a bass-tone chuckle that was quickly choked off. It solved the puzzle of how one voice could both whine and command so convincingly.

"Obilin informed me that your dressmaker had arrived," Pylomel said, obviously deciding that it was time to get to the point. "It is she I have come to see, not you, lady. Rassa, my beautiful girl, come with me."

"She will stay here," Zefra said, her voice still quite calm.

"By sending her here, her father has granted me certain . . . privileges, lady. I'm sure you understand."

Zefra made a tight, sharp sound that might have been a laugh. "I understand quite well, Lord. I have no quarrel with your pleasures. But the Celebration Dance is only two days away, and Rassa must make a gown for me. She will stay here in this apartment until the gown is complete to my satisfaction. Then you may have her."

"And when, dear lady," said Pylomel, "did you decide to attend the dance? The last time we discussed it, you denied your son the honor of your presence on this important occasion."

"I have thought better of it," Zefra said, and her voice took on a different tone, almost humble. "Indomel is my only child, after all. And now that I have acceded to your wishes, Lord, will you punish me by depriving me of the only dressmaker I trust to prepare my gown in the time left?"

A moment's silence. My hand tightened on the hilt of the sword, while I strained and waited to hear Pylomel's next words.

"Very well," he said at last. "She may stay—with this understanding. On the night of the celebration, after the dance, she will come to me." He laughed. "Perhaps that is appropriate, after all. It is a high occasion, and we will continue our celebration through the night. Is that not so, Rassa?

"Why, girl, you're trembling. Let me comfort you a moment."

I gritted my teeth, and told myself: *Zefra knows what she's doing, and Tarani isn't being hurt*. But as the silence stretched on, it changed to: *If he doesn't take his hands off her . . .*

"Better now, dear girl?" Pylomel's voice said, and he was answered by an indistinct murmur. "Then it is settled, Zefra. She will stay here until after the Celebration Dance—and it is your duty to see she remains. Is that clear?"

"Perfectly, Lord. Now, may we get on with the measuring? Time is very short."

"Certainly. And I will inform our son of your change of heart. Doubtless he will be overcome with joy."

The minute I heard the doors close, I ran out into the room and took Tarani into my arms. She sagged against me and shuddered.

13

"Did you see him?" Tarani asked. "Rikardon, I've never met anyone so...repulsive." She pulled away from me and faced Zefra. "Mother, how could you stand to be here...*with him*...all these years?"

"I had to be with him only a short time, dear," she answered, and turned away abruptly. Her voice came softly, bitterly, over her shoulder. "Only until I produced an heir." She seemed to shake herself, then began to pace about the room as she talked. "Since Indomel's birth, Pylomel has left me quite alone. I have even been spared the need to appear at official functions—though he did request my presence at the Celebration Dance."

"I've heard something of the celebration," I said. "But I don't understand what the occasion is."

"Indomel will be designated the next High Lord," Zefra said. "Oh, he won't have the position until Pylomel dies, but I wouldn't put it past the little fleason to assassinate his father, first chance he gets."

"You said Indomel is your son!" Tarani cried, shocked.

"The son of my body, Tarani. But Pylomel took him away *hours* after his birth, and he's trained him to be as devious and decadent and...I hate him almost as much as I hate Pylomel."

Tarani and I were both a little stunned at the violence of the outburst, but in the next moment, Zefra's voice was tender once again.

"You, my darling, are the daughter of my spirit as well as my body."

"Mother," Tarani said impulsively, "you must come with us when we leave Eddarta. You've no reason to stay here any longer, not to protect me or—Volitar."

"Yes, your young man told me that he is gone," Zefra said sadly, and once more mother and daughter embraced.

I didn't ask Tarani how she planned to get her mother out of there. Tarani's world and Zefra's world had been entirely separate until bare moments ago, yet the two women, so much alike physically, had formed an immediate affection for one another. I knew that if it were possible, Zefra would leave Eddarta with us. I could no more willingly leave her behind than I could leave Tarani.

But other things had to come first.

"Gharlas killed Volitar," I said, and Zefra and Tarani drew apart. "And he stole something which belongs to Tarani. That's why we've come—to get it back."

"Gharlas? Why would he kill Volitar?"

Tarani spoke, then, telling then Zefra about Gharlas. How he had blackmailed Volitar into duplicating gemstones, so that Gharlas could replace the treasures in Pylomel's vault, using the secret entrance Gharlas had found. How Volitar had fought to the last to protect Tarani from him. How we had confronted Gharlas in the workshop, and Tarani's display of power had proved her heritage.

"He knows who I am, Mother, and he could use that against you. Even if he hadn't killed Volitar, the threat to you would give me enough reason to be here."

I was startled when I got a good look at Zefra's face. There was sadness in it, and an odd glow that made me uneasy. I didn't know if it meant she was a little unbalanced—hardly an unreasonable occurrence, considering the peculiar life she lived—or if that light was anticipation of revenge on Gharlas.

"There are few here who would regret Gharlas's death," she said. "But he isn't in the city, as far as I know."

"He's on his way," I said. "Tomorrow—the day after at

the latest—he'll be here. We need your help to know where to find him."

Zefra smiled, and the odd light went away. "He is easily found; he lives in the last house, the one nearest the wall. Also the smallest." She laughed. "What sweet justice that the old passageway really does exist."

"You know about it?" Tarani asked. "Can we use it to get into his house unobserved?"

"No, child, for if it truly is Troman's Way, it connects only with the Council Chamber in the Lord Hall. There have always been rumors of its existence. Troman was a High Lord of an elder age, who believed in the semblance of discretion. He installed a succession of young women in that small house, and visited them while he was, supposedly, inspecting the treasure vault."

"Wasn't he afraid that the women would steal from him?" I asked.

"Indeed, he was. That's why he concealed the house entry so cleverly that none of the girls ever found it—or the many residents who have searched for it since. When he died, the secret died, which was just as well. There has never been a High Lord since Troman who bothered to conceal his . . . pleasures. It has been so long, now, that it's generally believed that Troman's Way was only a rumor."

"Well, if we can't use it, then it's not important," I said. "This Celebration Dance—will Gharlas be there?"

"If he has arrived by then, certainly. Attendance is mandatory." She smiled, and the strange light was back. "For everyone but me, that is."

"Then we'll plan to search the house that night."

"And if it isn't in the house?" Tarani asked.

"Then he'll have it on his person. We can wait for him to come back."

"Meanwhile," Zefra said, "I must do something about a new gown. Pylomel is nothing if not observant; if I wear an old gown, he will recognize it."

Tarani laughed—a beautiful sound. "Oh, that's not a problem, Mother. I *can* sew. Come and choose a fabric."

We spent the night and the next day in Zefra's apartment. At first, Tarani did most of the talking, her fingers busy with the soft, pale fabric which Zefra had chosen. I could hear the love and admiration in her voice when she talked of Volitar—his care of her, the things he believed in, his patience and skill as he mastered his new trade. Tarani spoke more diffidently of the Recorder's school which she had attended until age sixteen.

"Yes, I knew you had a strong mindpower the day you were born, Tarani, and I warned Volitar to watch for it to emerge."

"How did you know, so soon?" Tarani asked.

Zefra didn't answer immediately. "Even as an infant," she said at last, "your resemblance to me was apparent. I have a strong mind-gift, and it seemed possible that you would inherit that quality, also." She smiled. "You are very skilled at illusion, daughter. Did the Recorders teach you that?"

"No," Tarani said, and the skin of her cheeks seemed to shrink in on the bone structure.

She's trying to decide whether to tell Zefra about Molik, I realized. *Surely Zefra, of all people, would understand her drive and determination to get what she wanted—at any cost. But Tarani's still not comfortable with the memory.*

Even as those thoughts were flashing through my mind, Tarani had made her decision, and was speaking. "I worked for a while as a seamstress," she lied, "and when I had enough money, I organized an entertainment troupe."

She continued the story from there, and managed to tell it without mentioning Molik or his assassins. She dwelled mostly on the acts in the show, including her own. Once Zefra turned to me—the first time she addressed me directly—and asked me if I had seen the show. Tarani busied herself with her sewing, and I knew she was remembering that her performance had been a diversion, so that Molik's assassins would have a chance to kill me.

Is she afraid I'll tell the truth? I wondered, feeling a little hurt at her lack of trust. *Well, I will.*

"I have seen Tarani dance, Zefra," I answered. "There is nothing in this world more lovely."

"And how did you meet my daughter, Rikardon? Why are you helping her in her quest for revenge against Gharlas?"

"It is my quest, too," I said, then hesitated, searching for a plausible reason for my involvement.

But Zefra smiled and nodded, reached out to press my hand with her own for a moment. "You needn't try to hide the obvious, Rikardon. I have seen the love you share. Remember that I have known that kind of love, as well. I'm very glad that Tarani is not alone."

I didn't dare look at Tarani, and I noticed that she was quick to change the subject.

"Tell me about Volitar," Tarani pleaded. "What happened when you left Eddarta?"

Zefra sighed and shivered, but she remained silent for a moment that became more awkward as the silence continued. Finally, Tarani prompted her gently: "Mother?"

"You must be a little patient with me, child," Zefra said. "For eighteen years I have used every power at my command to keep hidden the story you have asked to hear."

"If it is too painful to remember now, Mother—"

"No, Tarani, I want you to know... about Volitar. But the story begins two years before I met him, when I was a child of Ruthanan—my birth family's name—and attending my first Gathering, an event which is held yearly to commemorate the safe arrival of the Seven Families in Eddarta. Attendance at the Gathering is not mandatory, but absences are noticed. Besides, there is much business done at the Gathering, where all Families are, for a time, equal.

"Some of that business concerns the children. Everyone who reached sixteen years of age during the previous year appears at the Gathering. In a year such as this, when the next High Lord attends the Gathering, it becomes a Celebration Dance, and the confirmation ceremony is performed on the following day.

"For most of the children, it is the first time they have

been seen by members of the other Families. It is here that the bargaining begins."

"Bargaining?" I asked. "For what?"

"For marriages," Zefra answered shortly. "It is required that everyone marry someone from another Family. One isn't obligated to marry at all, of course, but—again— failure to marry is regarded as suspicious, since it is everyone's duty to assure the continuance of the mind-gift."

Gharlas said that they were "breeding for the mind-gift," I remembered. Somehow, I didn't expect such a formalized, highest-bidder sort of situation.

"But mindpower wasn't all there is to be gained," Zefra went on bitterly. "A property trade usually goes along with a marriage bond, and the Lords look upon the Family children as marketable items."

"But after all these years, how can any individual claim to be from only one Family?" I asked.

"In every marriage, the woman—and her children— become members of the husband's Family: No, that's wrong," she amended. "They become the *property* of that Family, at least since Pylomel become High Lord, which happened two years after my first Gathering. He 'reformed' the property system by assigning all patronages held by Family members to the Family as a whole, and giving the Lords the power to assign rightful portions of their income to each household in the Family."

"Could he do that," Tarani asked, "without the *consent* of the other Lords?"

Zefra laughed. "My dear, he had no trouble winning their consent. In the first place, the system did need some kind of reforming. Originally the Families had been granted patronages that were localized—one farming area, one city area—and they had been assigned to the Family units living at that time. But after years of subdivision to heirs, and trading for beneficial marriages, it took ten full-time clerks to keep track of who was entitled to what revenue within each Family.

"In the second place, Pylomel was quick to recognize

that the other Lords shared his greedy temperament, and would see the opportunity for control as an opportunity for profit.

"In the third place," Zefra continued, "Pylomel included, as part of the agreement, that the High Lord would have the right to monitor each Lord's dispersal of patronage funds, and would be the final judge in any Family dispute. In this way, he gave the Families some promise of protection against greed, while unofficially assuring the Lords that he would support their decisions completely."

Zefra shook her head. "No, Pylomel had no trouble convincing the Lords to his 'reform proposal.' But to give them credit, they hadn't had the chance to know Pylomel by then. He was the youngest High Lord ever to take office! Did you know that? Some say, now, and very softly, that he arranged his father's death. But at eighteen, he had an impressive knowledge of the details of the system, and of the personalities of the individual Lords. What would have taken the old High Lord days of discussion and argument to settle, Pylomel could accomplish with only a few words."

I exchanged glances with Tarani. "Compulsion?" I asked. "Was he using his mindpower to convince them?"

Zefra nodded her head in a mock bow. "Very good, Rikardon. But you must remember that you are acquainted with someone with a strong mind-gift. We of the Seven Families, although the concept is never far from us, have rarely seen so powerful a mind as Pylomel's."

Suddenly I was very worried. "Gharlas said he was denied the accession because of his illegitimacy," I said, "but that he 'tested' *higher* than Pylomel."

14

"That's quite true," Zefra said. "Pylomel admitted to me that he showed only enough of his power during the final testing to assure that he would win the succession. And he was well aware of the effect it had on Gharlas; to this day he still laughs about it."

No wonder Gharlas hates Pylomel's tusks, I thought, feeling a kind of sympathy for the man, with full recognition of how ironic my reaction was. But something didn't make sense.

"Everything I've heard about Pylomel leads me to think he would have wanted to boast about his strength," I said. "He seems to enjoy controlling people. Why did he hide the extent of his power?"

"In that," Zefra said, "he had an excellent example from the previous generation. The mind-gift has been reappearing, ever more strongly, in recent times. Pylomel's father faced a High Lord candidate who showed a startling gift, and had no hesitation about using it. You must understand that all the official testing is done in private—the children don't see the performance of the other candidates. Well, *this* boy's power frightened the Lords. The story goes that he could read, as well as control, minds—the most rare of all mind-gifts. The Lords agreed to tamper with the test results, to keep the boy from gaining power.

"When they announced that Horinad, Pylomel's father, was to be the next High Lord, the boy understood immediately that he had been cheated. He stood up in the room where all the candidates waited for the results, denounced the Lords, and laid a suicide compulsion on all of them. Three were dead by the time the boy could be knocked unconscious."

"What happened to him?" Tarani asked.

"The remaining Lords had him killed, of course. So you see, Pylomel knew better than to frighten the Lords too early with the strength of his mind. He waited until he had the political power to support it, and he used it most subtly, until he began to believe that he is invulnerable."

"What are the tests like?" The question came from Tarani, but I was curious about the answer, too.

"There are two sets of tests," Zefra said. "The early one is given to all children, not just those who may be eligible to become High Lord."

"To the girls, as well?" I asked.

"Yes, certainly, to the girls," Zefra answered bitterly. "The mother-buyers have to know how much power we have to offer as breeding stock." Then she laughed. "Not that it does them much good. The girls learn about the system, early on, and regularly cheat on those tests."

"How can you show more power than you have?" Tarani wondered.

I answered her. "Not more—less. Am I right, Zefra?"

"Exactly right again, Rikardon. What mindpower we do have, is our only protection; we prefer to keep it a secret.

"To answer your question, Tarani, those tests are very like the ones you probably had at Recorder's school. Throwing mondeana and calling the results before they settle. Identifying shapes held out of sight. That sort of thing."

Like the star/circle/wavy-line cards used in ESP research in Ricardo's world, I thought. *But they don't consider that kind of sensitivity, which would seem to be very common, to be the same thing as direct thought reading. Maybe that's because of the probability factor. The Gandalarans may think that the right answer about the cards or the mondeana comes through the comparison/ computation link with the All-Mind, rather than as a message from the mind of another person. While actual understanding of another's thoughts . . .*

Hello. There's a new idea. If the All-Mind consists of the memories or personalities (depending on your viewpoint) of all past individuals, are living individuals part of it? Or can they just "talk" to it, in varying degrees, on a conscious or subconscious level?

That would put direct thought reading or control between living people in a wholly different category. And even here in Eddarta, where they claim to value mind-gifts, that power scares them. Maybe that should be: especially here in Eddarta, where the Lords know it can happen, and can threaten their own political power.

"The second test is more complex, but basically the same skills, I think," Zefra was saying. "The first set is given at age twelve, the second at age fifteen—only to High Lord candidates. There is a third and final test given to the next High Lord as part of the ceremony which names him successor. He must read the Bronze."

She said that as if "the Bronze" were some kind of sacred document, I thought. Yet, as far as I know, the Gandalarans don't believe in any sort of God. They think they understand the All-Mind, and everyone has access to it.

Oh, well, I'm still a stranger here, as I am reminded every day.

"But I have strayed far from the story I was telling," Zefra continued. "Pylomel instituted his 'reform' for only one reason—to get me for his wife. I know that sounds immodest, but it is true, and it should tell you to what extent he will go to achieve his slightest wish.

"I met him on the night of my first Gathering. He was eighteen, and the designated successor. I have said that my own gift is fairly strong—I sensed the corruption of his personality, and could hardly bear to have him near me, even for the time required for a single dance. I knew how he felt about me, of course. Ill with fear and repulsion, I left the celebration early.

"I waited up for my father, and ran to meet him when

102

he came home. He held me tightly as he spoke of the bargaining that Pylomel's father had initiated.

"'I've always promised you that your marriage would have your own consent, Zefra,' he told me. 'Since I couldn't find you to discuss it, I compromised. I told them that I would not consider you marriageable until you were eighteen. But, daughter, it is an honor to be sought by the next High Lord. Would such a match have your consent?'

"I told him the truth then—that I would rather die than let Pylomel touch me. And he promised me that Pylomel would not have me—not if it cost my father his fortune.

"Two years later, Pylomel's father was dead, and Pylomel was High Lord. He approached my father again, about a month before my eighteenth birthday, and was again refused. The next day, I found my father assassinated in his bed."

Zefra's voice had become soft and fragile as she had talked of her own father. Now she shook herself and continued in a stronger voice.

"It is our custom that, if a marriage bond is not confirmed before a girl turns eighteen, she is free to make her own choice. I had seen Pylomel a few times—at obligatory social functions, in chance meetings—and he knew that I would never come to him willingly. I think now that it was only my repeated refusals which kept him so determined to have me. My father's brother had the power to make such a bond, but after I told him the whole story, he, too, refused Pylomel's offer.

"That's when Pylomel invented his brilliant 'reform', which gave the Lord the right to manipulate matters of property. The day before I was eighteen, *I* was still 'property', and my Lord traded me for three grain farms and a butchery."

We were silent a moment, Tarani and I feeling the tragedy of the young girl whose life was completely out of her control.

"Is that when you ran away?" Tarani asked at last.

"Soon afterward," Zefra said. "Pylomel insisted that I be given quarters in his home—these very rooms, in fact—

until the wedding celebration could be held. He . . . visited me, one evening, asking . . .

"I was unwise. Not content with a simple refusal, I let my hatred of him show, saying that I would perform that duty only when it was legally necessary.

"Of course, he was furious—and determined to break me down, one way or another. The way he chose was humiliation. He ordered that a commemorative coin be issued for our wedding, but that it display only *his* face. He decreed that each of his landservants would, out of the joy of the occasion, purchase one of those coins at twice its value. Then he sent *me* into Eddarta's streets to 'sell' the coins. He succeeded this far—" She clenched her fists, and a tremor ran along her arms. "*I was humiliated!*"

Zefra became aware of her tension, and made a visible effort to relax, taking several deep breaths before she continued.

"I had rid myself of three quarters of the coins when I came to Volitar's shop. As always, I left the guards outside the shop and went in alone. There was something special about Volitar, who was nearly as old as my own father. I had seen a lot of grief and resignation in far younger men, but in Volitar I saw a spark of defiance. It seemed the most natural thing in the world to tell him . . . everything. Without another word, without once looking backward, he took my hand and led me out the rear door of his shop, then out of Eddarta."

She smiled, and there was a softness in her face we hadn't seen before. "At first, I didn't love Volitar. We both understood that we had chosen to do something together that we had been too frightened to try while we were alone. We took pleasure in being together, and in being free, even though the trip was a hard one for us. It was so ironic—I still had Pylomel's gold coins, but we didn't dare spend them, for fear of being traced.

"But once we were in Dyskornis, and he had found a means to support us, and I began to believe, really *believe* that we might get away with it—then my gratitude to Volitar changed to love. When you were born, Tarani, I thought there could never be two people more happy than Volitar and I. Even when Pylomel's agents found me, I could be happy that I was alone, and that they didn't know about Volitar and . . . about you, dear. I let Pylomel believe that he had won what he wanted—that I had hated the outside world, but I had been too proud to return on my own. He was satisfied, and I was content. I gave him my body, but kept my mind closed to him—I have that much power."

"Didn't that make trouble for you?" I asked.

"On the contrary," Zefra answered, "Pylomel is so sure of his own power that he doesn't suspect mine. We discussed his power only once, but I remember what he said. 'I don't read thoughts,' he told me. 'But I can sense a person's attitude. I know when I'm being lied to,' he said, not realizing that I was lying to him at that very moment. I think that he doesn't realize he *can't* sense anything from me, but his unknowing reliance on *only* my words and actions makes him nervous around me. As I said, he has left me to myself since Indomel's birth."

"Yet he has kept you here," Tarani said, "in fine state."

"Do you think he would put me aside for another wife?" Zefra asked. "No. An agreeable, undemanding wife affords him a shelter under which he can pursue his other interests. And Indomel is my son—to get rid of me without declaring the boy illegitimate, he would have to kill me. Pylomel still takes some pleasure in my imprisonment, and in what it represents—the memory of his hardest-won victory. Or so he thinks.

"But surely that's enough about me. I was asking, too, where you and Rikardon met, Tarani."

"In Thagorn," Tarani said. "My troupe was performing—"

"*Thagorn?*" Zefra demanded, startling Tarani into missing a stitch. "Isn't that the city where those traitors, the Sharith, live?"

"Traitors?" Tarani repeated.

"Yes, traitors! It was because of them that Harthim had to leave the golden halls of Kä and bring the Seven Families here to Eddarta!"

To say that Tarani and I were surprised by Zefra's challenge would be to understate our reaction—then, or in the next moment, when Zefra laughed, showing some embarrassment.

"But how foolish of me to judge them today by what they did generations ago! One has trouble seeing any kinship between Harthim's enlightened leadership and Pylomel's self-serving, greedy manipulation of the Seven Families. Why should one expect the Sharith to remain the enemies of the Kingdom, or ask them to bear that ancient blame?

"Enlightened leadership"? I thought, incredulously. *I guess it does depend on your viewpoint. But I wonder if that was Volitar's opinion, too, of the last King.*

"So," Zefra continued, "you were saying that you met this young man while your troupe was performing in Thagorn?"

I answered her: "I was visiting a friend in Thagorn when Tarani's show was to be given. My friend invited me to attend, and introduced us after the dance was over. As I was ready, by then, to continue my journey to Dyskornis, Tarani invited me to travel with her caravan, for reasons of safety. We were friends by the time we reached Dyskornis, and I went with her to meet Volitar. We found him being tortured by Gharlas—the rest you know."

"This thing which Gharlas has—what is it?" Zefra asked.

Tarani looked at me, and I happened to move my hand across my home-made leather belt. I grabbed the belt and the idea at the same time.

"Volitar still had all the gold coins," I told Zefra. "Gharlas stole them. Even if they were only ordinary coins, Tarani would be entitled to recover them. Now that we know what they mean, however . . ."

"Yes," Zefra agreed. "Yes, you must get them back. I will do all I can to help you."

15

Tarani stayed with Zefra nearly every moment on that day. I was occasionally exiled to an inner room, as meals were delivered, or as Zefra received or sent messages. Thono, the young girl who had let us into the apartment the day before, came and went a few times in the morning, and arrived again in the afternoon with the news we wanted to hear: Gharlas was in Eddarta.

I didn't have a chance to speak to Tarani alone until that night. Zefra had wished us goodnight, and we were in the room which Tarani's mother had given us to share—without asking our approval of the arrangement. The night before, we had been too exhausted by tension to be bothered by the awkwardness of the situation; we had merely pulled the side-by-side pallets a little way apart, and slept.

Tonight I was thinking: *We spent night after night in the desert, alone, and never felt this tension. What is it about being in a room together that gives a situation sexual overtones?*

Quit fooling yourself, I told myself then. *In the desert, our feelings for one another were hidden. Now they're out in the open—so obvious, in fact, that Zefra read them easily. How was she to know that Tarani and I haven't yet expressed those feelings in the traditional way? The tension won't dissipate until we do.*

It was Tarani who broke the uncomfortable silence. "Thank you, Rikardon, for—" She laughed a little. "—for lying to my mother."

"What you want her to know is your own affair, Tarani," I said. "I have the feeling she isn't telling you everything, either."

Tarani looked hurt, and worried. "Yes, I have had the same thought. Rikardon, I do not understand why it should be this way. I thought I had come to terms with the memory of Molik, yet I found I could not tell Zefra about him. Why not?"

Maybe Antonia wouldn't let you, I thought. *I think she was right*.

"For the same reason you didn't tell Zefra about the Ra'ira, Tarani. You don't know her that well, yet. You may be as closely related as two people can get, but that doesn't mean that both of you will automatically accept each other without judgment. I saw how shocked you were when Zefra reacted against the Sharith."

She began to pace slowly around the room. "I have asked her more than once to come with us when we leave, but she has never given me a definite answer. She always turns the discussion to another topic." She faced me, held her arms out in question. "Do *you* think she wants to come with us?"

"I can't answer for her, Tarani. But if she wants to come, we'll do everything we can to take her with us."

"Thank you," she said, and the tension intensified. She seemed to be waiting for something. For me.

I wanted her with an aching need, but the question was still there: Which woman did I want? The sensitive young girl who was, even now, undergoing the emotional upheaval of the first meeting with her mother? Or the worldly woman, not much older in years, but rich in experience and knowledge of people?

I opened my arms, and she came into them. I held the body that belonged to two different women, and gave a silent prayer for patience and wisdom.

After a moment, Tarani barely whispered: "It isn't time yet, is it?"

I pressed the slim, supple body even closer to me, then

released her . . . them. I hoped she heard my regret as I said: "Goodnight, Tarani."

I blew out the candle in the lamp, and we settled in to sleep. I simply lay down in my clothes, but I heard movement and rustling that told me Tarani was taking off the dress she had borrowed from Rassa's wardrobe. The sound soothed me, rather than excited me. It was such a natural thing to do, and so completely a sign of trust, that it brought back the feeling of uninvolved companionship we had shared in the desert. The ache abated, and I was able to sleep.

My rest was fitful, and in the many wakeful moments of the night, I blamed the inactivity of the previous day. After our routine of hard physical activity, the enforced idleness had all my muscles complaining of disuse.

But Tarani's day had been more strenuous—hurrying to finish the gown, talking to Zefra, switching Rassa's illusion on and off—and the rhythm of her breathing spoke of a deep, restful sleep.

So it was I, and not Tarani, who heard the tapping and scratching in the early hours of the morning. I got up, followed the sound, and opened the latticed windows that faced the garden. A heavy object struck me in the chest, and I staggered backward, trying to support the weight so that it wouldn't fall.

It flapped and hooted and butted at my chest. "Lonna!" I whispered. "Yes, I'm glad to see you, too. Now hush, or you'll wake Tarani."

Finally I held the large bird cradled in my arm, and stroked her back and the tips of her long wings. She twisted her neck until the downward hook at the end of her beak dug affectionately into my shoulder, then just enjoyed the attention.

She didn't have a message tied to her anywhere. The bird had a surprisingly large vocabulary of words she could understand, but I didn't feel like playing "twenty questions" at that time of the morning—especially since Tarani's limited psychic link with Lonna could retrieve any message easily, once she woke up.

109

Tarani did awaken at first light, and nearly scared me to death by sitting straight up in bed and calling out: "Lonna!" I had been sitting with my back against the wall, half-dozing with the bird resting in my lap. The bird jumped away from me, wings flapping, with such force that I was sent sprawling to one side. When I righted myself, I saw Tarani, naked from the waist up, trying to hug Lonna while laughing at the bird's happy antics.

I turned my face away, filled with a need that had nothing to do with Tarani. I wanted to be with Keeshah, so badly that I could feel his fur in the palms of my hands. I reached out to him mentally, and thrilled to feel his joy at the contact.

When together? he asked me.

Tonight, with any luck, I told him. *Wait until after dark, then come as close to the city as you can. When we leave, we'll be in a hurry.*

Keeshah must have sensed what I wasn't saying: *If we get out of here alive.*

I will help! came his determined thought.

There is nothing you can do, Keeshah, I told him. *Strength won't win this round. It will all be easier for me, if I know you're waiting.*

I will wait, he agreed reluctantly, then amended it: *For a time.*

I want a promise from you, Keeshah—one that will not be easy to keep.

What? he asked, the feeling of suspicion clear in his thought.

If I am killed, I want you to take Tarani to safety. Let that be your first duty, even above avenging my death. Do you agree?

There was a short silence, just the quiet awareness of our link. Then, with little warning, Keeshah's mind swept into mine, forming the close, intensely personal contact we had shared before. He withdrew nearly as quickly, leaving me a little breathless, but in that moment of contact, he had learned what he wanted to know—that my

110

request wasn't just a whim, or a mere favor to Tarani, but that her life was infinitely precious to me.

I will do it, he promised. *But don't die.*

I laughed out loud. *Thank you, Keeshah. I'll try my best.*

I broke the contact to find Tarani dressed, holding Lonna, and smiling at me. "Keeshah?" she asked.

I nodded. "He'll be waiting outside the city for us tonight."

"So will Ronar," she said. "Thymas sent Lonna to tell us that he's in Eddarta."

It was comforting to know that Thymas was here. Tarani and I discussed procedure, and decided that it was important for us to remain hidden until time to act; we didn't dare risk a meeting with Thymas. So we sent a message with Lonna:

> We are in the Inner City, will move quietly against
> G tonight. Wait near city gate, be ready to distract
> guard. May be late, T will tell you when.
> R.

While Tarani worked furiously on the gown, Zefra and I conferred about the layout of the Harthim section, and the best way to get to Gharlas's house unseen. She sketched as much of the house's floorplan as she could remember. When we had discussed everything she or I thought might be helpful to us tonight, I sat back from the table we were using and said: "Tarani wants you to come with us, Zefra, but you won't say yes or no. Don't you think she deserves an answer?"

Tarani, who was seated on the window ledge, working by the window, let the pale yellow dress settle into her lap.

"There will be so many people at the dance, Mother," she said. "It will be easy for you to slip away. I'll let you know when."

A light compulsion, I thought. *That's what she'll use on Thymas, too. It's not as efficient as a walkie-talkie, but it makes a pretty useful signal device.*

111

Zefra sighed, and closed her eyes for a moment. "Tarani, I cannot say how much it has meant to me, seeing you grown, hearing that Volitar loved me to the last, and respected my wishes for you." She got up and walked over to the window, sat beside Tarani, and took her hands. "It would be wonderful if we could be together for the rest of our lives, daughter. But why must I go with you? Couldn't you stay here with me?"

"But Mother, you've said that it would enrage Pylomel if he ever learned you have deceived him all these years! It would be dangerous for both of us, if I stayed."

"No one need know you are here," Zefra said quietly.

Tarani stared at her mother. "You mean that I should stay in these rooms with you, and hide whenever someone comes in? I couldn't live like that, Mother, not like a hunted animal . . ."

Her voice died as Zefra's point hit home.

"I did live like that once," Zefra said. "It takes a special kind of strength, Tarani, and I have used all I had. I am comfortable here, and I have more influence in Lord City than it seems I do. Just by being here, I am proof that Pylomel has his limits. The Lords sometimes ask my advice on important issues, and I give them what guidance I can on how best to deal with the High Lord."

She stood up and came over to me. "Take the coins back from Gharlas," she told me. "Take Tarani and the gold far from here, and—mind this, now—have the gold melted and recast. If any one of those coins turns up outside Eddarta, it will be noticed.

"Even deducting the cost of the metallurgy service," she said, "you will have a small fortune. I hope and trust that you—" Her voice broke; she had to clear her throat before she could go on. "—that you and Tarani will have a happy, peaceful life together."

Tarani let the dress fall to the floor as she rushed over and threw her arms around her mother. They clung to one another, talking at the same time, sharing the misery of the parting that seemed so close now. It was another of those times when I was merely a spectator, and again I

112

withdrew from them as a purely automatic reaction. Before I knew it, I was alone, standing at our bedroom window, looking out over the garden.

Tarani came in a few minutes later and said: "She asked me to call her away from the dance tonight, anyway, so that we can say good-bye one more time. I said I would do it—I hope that's all right."

"Of course it is, Tarani. Let's take a few seconds and go over what she told me about the house where Gharlas will be staying..."

16

The room we had first entered was merely a wide hallway with chairs. It led into a large, private sitting room which connected with several other rooms, including a tiled balcony where meals were served. We were in the private sitting room now, and Tarani was adjusting a fold of the gown while Zefra admired herself in a polished-brass mirror.

"It's lovely," Zefra said, "truly lovely. Rassa herself could have done no better."

A knock sounded on the outer door, and before any of us could react, we heard it open. I made a dash for the bedroom door and pushed it nearly shut after me, just as the inner door opened and I heard a booted step strike the tile which floored the private sitting room.

"Obilin!" Zefra said. "How dare you enter my apartment without permission?"

"I have a higher permission, lady," said the small man's voice, heavy and insolent. "I am to escort your dressmaker to her new apartment."

"My bargain with the High Lord specified that Rassa would be available to him *after* the Celebration Dance," Zefra argued.

"And *his* bargain—as he explained it to me, lady—was that you would keep the dressmaker until your gown was completed. Which it is. And quite lovely, too, if I may say it.

"The High Lord sent me to assure Rassa's safe arrival in her new quarters."

Zefra put on a good show of fuming and fussing. "Does he think I would go back on my word? You may return to him, Obilin, and assure him that Rassa will be awaiting him after the dance. *I* will see to it, as I promised."

"Sorry," Obilin said, and I could almost hear him grinning. "There is a complication—an intruder."

"What?"

"A man named Lakad hired on as a guardsman two days ago, and then disappeared. We have no idea where he is, but he may still be in the area. The Guard has been alerted to watch for him, but the High Lord thinks it wise that all . . . ladies . . . should be . . ."

His voice trailed off like the noise in a toy as its batteries finally give up. The short fur on the back of my neck lifted as I heard Zefra speak. Her voice was like a whip of ice.

She said: "Obilin, you have done as the High Lord commanded. Rassa is in the apartment prepared for her, awaiting Pylomel. What's more, you, yourself, located the intruder, and killed him. You will call off the watch. Do you understand all that?"

"Yes." A murmur.

"Then return to Pylomel. When you see him, you will act and think normally. You will remember what I have told you as if it truly happened, and you will not remember that I spoke to you at all. You came here, collected Rassa with no trouble, and delivered her as ordered. Go now."

I came out of the bedroom as Obilin reached the outer door of the entrance room; he had gone through the inner door without bothering to close it after himself. He was moving slowly, just as you'd imagine someone would move, under the control of another mind. I went through the formal sitting room to close the outside door, then returned, closing the inner door as I came through it.

I couldn't read Tarani's face, but Zefra's was openly triumphant. "Now you see what I have hidden from Pylomel all these years. My mind-gift is as strong as

115

his—even stronger, in some ways. Tonight, when he goes to Rassa drunk and lustful, and finds an empty apartment, I will send him into unconsciousness and give him a memory of all he wanted to experience. And he will never guess the truth."

"It's time for us to go," I said, taking Tarani's hand and pulling her toward the doorway. "We need to be in position to see Gharlas leave the house."

Zefra moved to Tarani and hugged her. "Be careful, darling. And remember to call me—I must see you one more time before you leave."

"I won't forget, Mother," Tarani said.

As we had planned, Zefra called the two guards inside, on the pretext of moving a heavy piece of furniture. Tarani and I, cloaked by her illusion, stepped out into the main house and left the apartment which had been our home for the past two and a half days.

We moved cautiously through the twisting hallways. Twice, it was necessary for Tarani to conceal us through illusion, as guards or servants walked by. Though it seemed a long trip, it was no more than five minutes before we stepped out into the fragrant garden. Only then could we talk about what we had seen.

"She *enjoyed* setting that compulsion, Rikardon," Tarani whispered, shuddering. "What would Volitar have thought, seeing her like that? How could this have happened to the woman who ran away from exactly that kind of power?"

"Tarani—" I began, but she hadn't really stopped talking. She gripped my arms.

"Please, Rikardon, you read people better than I do. I cannot leave her unless I understand how this . . . corruption could have happened to her."

"All right," I said, drawing her into the concealing shadow of the wall of the house. The sun hadn't set yet, but brilliant hues of red and orange had claimed the sky.

"Here's what I think," I told Tarani. "First, Zefra had a strong gift to begin with; she admitted she used it when she and Volitar escaped. Second, she's been virtually a prisoner for sixteen years, and her power was the only thing that gave her some control of her circumstances. Not to mention a touch of revenge against Pylomel, who created the prison for her.

"And third, the use of power is addictive, Tarani. Zefra's has become almost second nature—she has used it on me twice."

"On *you*?" she demanded. "When? Why did you not tell me?"

"Because I didn't realize it until she showed us how strong she is. Twice, when you and she were together, I was suddenly somewhere else, with no memory of how I got there. She probably didn't even know she was doing it."

She thought for a moment, while I kept a nervous watch for wandering guards. I didn't feel we really had time for this discussion, but I knew Tarani was right—until she had it settled in her mind, she wouldn't be able to concentrate fully on Gharlas.

Finally she sighed and said: "She wants us to think she will stay behind to help the Lords against Pylomel. But that is not the true reason, is it?"

"For what it's worth, Tarani, I think she really believes what Volitar taught you—that it is wrong to control another person's life or mind. She sees herself as defending Volitar's viewpoint."

"But she *has* to see it that way, does she not?" Tarani said bitterly. "To justify using the methods that Volitar despised." She shook herself sharply. "As you said, Rikardon, Zefra and I are strangers to one another. I cannot stand in judgment of her—she accepted this life of horror for my sake. But now . . . I feel less grief for leaving her. She and her power belong here, where the only people who can be hurt are those who inflict hurt."

I sensed a change in mood, the shrugging off of her sadness. "So now—the Ra'ira."

It was night by the time we slipped into a brushy area in front of Gharlas's house, which stood far back in the Harthim area, close to the outer wall of the city. Zefra's information had been invaluable in finding it; many of the homes looked alike in the dimness beyond the lamp-lit walkway. The timing, too, was perfect; we had been waiting less than ten minutes before Gharlas came out of the double entry doors and passed us, walking toward the Family entrance.

He was wearing dark clothes—a soft tunic and loose trousers, covered by an embroidered, hip-length vest cinched at the waist with a dark-jeweled belt. The dark colors accentuated his extreme height and paleness. When he walked between the marble pillars which supported the lamps, he seemed to be only a floating face and hands.

Tarani tensed as he passed us, and her hand went to the sword she had smuggled into Lord City inside a bolt of fabric. We were both dressed to travel, in tunic and desert-style trousers that tied at waist and ankle to keep out the salty dust. I kept my hand on my sword, too, and wished that it were Rika. I realized that part of my gladness to have Thymas close by was the prospect of getting Serkajon's steel sword back into my hands.

When Gharlas was out of sight, Tarani and I went around to the back of his house and slipped inside. *Good thing doors aren't locked in Lord City,* I thought. *I guess that's because everybody's so busy milking their landservants that they don't have time to steal from one another. Except Gharlas, that is.*

We lit some lamps, glad the house was in a secluded location. We were in a kitchen area—long unused, by the look of it, which was a relief. I had wondered about servants. If he had any, they didn't seem to be around.

We did a quick search of the exposed shelves and the reachable cabinets, then moved through a double doorway into a dining area. Another cursory search, and we passed into a sitting room that was really a huge hallway. Like the midhall in Raithskarian architecture, this one huge room ran the full length of the house, right down its center. Matching, marble-topped tables stood at strategic points. Only two lamps had been left burning, so that the entire room was very dimly lit. There was very little furniture—a

118

chair or two—to cover up the intricate geometric pattern of the floor tiles.

We were standing in a short hallway that led to the kitchen/dining area through which we had just come. Hulking darknesses at intervals on either side of the room seemed to be hallways that led from this main room to other living areas of the house. Between those entry areas, the walls were covered with thick tapestries, their scenes concealed from us by the dim light.

Pretty fancy, I thought. *Just what I would have expected from Gharlas. But spooky, with those flickering lamps. The place gives me the willies.*

Our plan was logical: first, make sure the Ra'ira wasn't in the house; next wait for Gharlas to return. Neither Tarani nor I seriously believed that Gharlas would let the jewel out of his possession for an instant, but we had to consider the possibility, if only because it was so unlikely.

But all the logic in the world isn't worth one good, gut-seizing hunch.

"This is too easy," I told Tarani, fighting the panic that was suddenly clutching at me. "Let's get out of here, right now."

"So soon, my friends? Why, you've only just arrived."

There it was—one hunch full-grown into one dangerous situation. Gharlas had appeared from behind the tapestry that hung beside the big, doubled front doors.

17

Tarani drew her sword and started for him, but I grabbed her.

"Bastard," she snarled at Gharlas.

In a world where women *knew* when they could be made pregnant, the word was a weighty curse, and maligned the mother as well as the child. In our last encounter with Gharlas, Tarani had used the epithet to distract him, but he wasn't going to be baited this time. His long, lean form seemed to ripple and he smiled as the word ran around the room in whispering echoes. Gharlas's smile wasn't the sort of thing you wanted to remember in the middle of the night. It creased his face and never touched the cold light that shimmered behind his eyes.

"Welcome to Eddarta, dear friends," he said. "It will be most beneficial to your future health if you will put down your swords. *Now!*"

Out of the dark hallways stepped swords with lots of husky muscle attached. It looked like Gharlas had selected the biggest and meanest of Pylomel's Guard.

So this is the payoff for all those "extra benefits", I thought. I recognized one of the men. Worse, he recognized me.

"You should have told me this was the guy, Gharlas," he said, stepping toward us from the hallway directly opposite the one we were blocking. "I caught a lot of grief for letting him into the city. It's gonna be a pleasure to kill him."

"*Stop, Sendar!*" Gharlas shouted. The big man did stop, but didn't quit leering at me like I was somebody's dinner.

"Death is very close to you right now, my friends," Gharlas said, his voice oily. "You know what I want. Give it to me."

I could almost feel the duplicate Ra'ira grow warm in the pouch hanging from my gold-lined belt. It was the real reason Gharlas had killed Volitar. Not everyone knew about the Ra'ira's special qualities, but nearly everyone did know it as a symbol of the Kingdom. In the process of forging a glass duplicate for the gem, Volitar had made *two* replicas. Gharlas had taken one of them to Raithskar with the intention of replacing the real one, and had later seen his accidental loss of the phony jewel as a blessing. He had realized that there must be no question, when the time came for him to reveal himself as King, that he did possess the only true Ra'ira. The existence of the second duplicate, the glass bauble I carried in my pouch, had taken him to Dyskornis. Volitar, having hidden it with his other greatest treasure, the letter from Zefra, had died without revealing either.

I glanced at Tarani, and saw the same determination on her face that I myself felt. We had come too many miles to back down now. Either we would leave here with the Ra'ira, or . . .

"How did you know we were going to be here?" I asked Gharlas. I was stalling for time, and he knew it. But he thought he was in control, and he had already shown us a tendency to boast. Not a modest guy, our Gharlas.

"Simple deduction," Gharlas said. "Hardly worth mentioning. The first thing I heard, when I arrived, was the rumor of an intruder calling himself Lakad. If you were here, so was she—and I knew what you wanted. *My* exceptional mind didn't have to guess when you would try to get it. I invited my friends here tonight, pretended to leave, and returned by the front door while you were scratching for lamps in the kitchen."

Markasset used that alias when Gharlas hired him to guard the caravan. Stupid. STUPID! I scolded myself.

But there's no help for that stupidity now. I concentrated, tried to remember our encounter in Dyskornis, searched for a weakness. Then I had it. His weakness was the same as his strength. The Ra'ira.

"I see that the female companionship you've been providing to the guards was money well spent," I said. "Got them to do the messy, dangerous work for you, haven't you? I see you prefer muscle to brains—otherwise Sendar wouldn't be here."

"Shut up," warned Sendar. "Gharlas, you want me to make him quiet?"

"That might be *just* what Gharlas wants, Sendar. Because he may be just a little bit worried that I'll tell you what this is all about. You see, he stole a jewel from Raithskar called—"

"*KILL HIM!*" Gharlas shouted, and Sendar leaped forward, his sword descending in a two-handed arc that would have split me in two—*if* I'd stood still.

But I had ducked around Sendar, and was running straight for Gharlas, scattering or jumping over furniture as it got in my way. Out of the corner of my eye, I saw Tarani slash at the big man's back, as his unresisted blow sent his swordtip clanging against the tile flooring. I was too busy to see more than that, because two other guards rushed out to intercept me before I could reach Gharlas.

These two were used to working as a team; one aimed high, the other low. I blocked the sword aimed for my head, jumped, and aimed a kick at the head of the guy swinging the lower blade. He flinched backward and missed his aim.

I heard footsteps behind me, and did some quick calculations. Six hallways opened into that room, and there had been a man in all but the one we had come through. That meant there were at least five guards—maybe more. Even if Tarani were calling Thymas in as reinforcement . . .

It doesn't look hopeful for the good guys, I thought.

I will help. Keeshah's thought struck me an instant before his mind merged with mine.

The Gandalaran who had been Markasset was a strong

and skillful fighter. In the first, awkward days of my residence in his body, Markasset's trained reflexes had saved me more than once. But there had been an occasion, like this one, where the odds were against me and Keeshah had been unable to join the fight physically. He had saved me then, as he was trying to do now, by lending me some of his abilities.

The effect of Keeshah's help was a drastic reduction of my reaction time. I had no greater strength and, in fact, no quicker reactions. What I had was the giant cat's *alertness* to sound, scent, and sight clues that were beyond Markasset's normal ability to interpret quickly. Keeshah's mind accepted the stimuli of *my* surroundings, as perceived by *my* senses. Because of the close joining of our minds, as soon as he interpreted, I had the knowledge necessary to guide my reactions.

So I knew, from the slightly differing odors, that there were only five men in the room. These two were trying to keep me away from Gharlas. From the sounds behind me, I could tell that Tarani was fighting Sendar, and the other two men were coming after me.

They don't know it yet, I thought fiercely, *but they just made a BAD choice*.

That was another thing Keeshah gave me. Spirit. When we were together in this special way, we *loved* a good fight.

I gauged the distance of the men behind me, and waited to hear the intake of breath that signaled a blow was about to be delivered. Then I whirled and ducked between them, running toward Tarani, and leaving them to scramble out of the way of their own swords.

That's your second mistake, guys, I thought, as I saw Tarani bring the big man down by slashing into his thigh, and then finish him. *You underestimated the lady*.

I turned to make a stand against the four guards, but Gharlas was smarter than that. "Go after the girl, you fools!"

Tarani was on her way to join me, but two of the guards broke past me to block her.

Damn you, Gharlas! I thought. *You think I'll leave myself vulnerable in order to protect Tarani. What you don't know is, she's worth any two men in a fight.*

But as my opponents and I circled and feinted, I caught glimpses of Tarani's struggle. It seemed more desperate than mine—I saw a couple of last-minute blocking moves that just barely saved her life.

What's going on? I wondered. *It's almost as though she can't control her own muscles...*

"Gharlas, you *bastard*," I yelled, as the truth struck home. He was using his mindpower to slow her down.

In Dyskornis, Tarani had proved that she could break through Gharlas's paralyzing control, given time. Part of her resistance came from her own mindpower, but I knew now that she could resist, partly, for the same reason I could—the non-Gandalaran portion of her mind was less susceptible.

Pressed as she was with immediate physical threat, she couldn't afford the concentration necessary to block Gharlas's power entirely. The paralysis trick had surprised us last time; this time, her natural resistance kept her moving, and the weight of his power kept her fractionally, dangerously slower than she needed to be. It might have had the same effect on me, but he had chosen Tarani for his target. First because, of the two of us, she was the weaker fighter. Second because he was counting on Tarani's predicament distracting me from my own problems.

It was working.

I snapped back into focus in time to knock aside a thrust aimed at my throat, but I was too late to dodge the other man's wild, hopeful slash, and the point of his blade cut a short gash on the left side of my chest.

The burning pain helped me to concentrate; I told myself I couldn't help Tarani until I got rid of these two.

Under the onslaught of these two men, I had been backing toward one of the long side walls, and I had about two feet to go before I wouldn't have room to breathe, much less fight.

Do something, I told myself, remembering one of Ricardo's favorite mottoes, *even if it's wrong.*

124

Getting myself pinned had lost me most of the advantages of Keeshah's help, but the eager, feisty presence of his mind in mine gave me a different kind of help—inspiration.

I took a deep breath and offered my best imitation of the roar of an angry sha'um.

Everybody paused for a second or two, startled by the unexpected noise. Everybody, that is, except me. I took a quick step backward, dropped my sword, clenched both hands in the fabric of the ceiling-high tapestry that covered the wall, and yanked the heavy stitchery down. As it came loose, I spun around and sent it sailing at the two guards who, recovered from their moment of surprise, were barely two paces away from me.

The weight of the thing sent them staggering; one corner flipped up to block their vision, and another whipped around behind them. I grabbed up my sword again as one of the guys tripped and fell. The other one was so busy trying not to get dragged down with him that he didn't see me coming. In another few seconds, both of them were out of action.

I jumped over them and ran to help Tarani, who was being pressed into the corner furthest from Gharlas by her two guards. She was fighting grimly, with sword and mind; every muscle of her face and body seemed wire-tight. I roared as I ran and one guard, distracted, looked around. Tarani thrust her sword through the left side of his chest. His eyes went blank, still staring at me, as he collapsed to the floor.

The pull on her sword sent Tarani to her knees, and the last guard closed in on her. I was one jump away from him, my sword raised and ready—and Gharlas turned his power on me.

My body completed the running step that had been in progress, but instead of striking the blow I planned, I skidded past Tarani and the guard without having time to swing my sword. I slammed heavily into the wall. The impact sent the sword flying from my sluggish hand. I turned around, and pushed away from the wall toward the fighting pair. It was like trying to swim through treacle, and inside I was screaming in frustration.

Tarani let go of the hilt of her sword to reach up with both hands; she grabbed the man's sword wrist and hung on. He wasn't as big as Sendar had been, but big enough. He couldn't pry Tarani's clutching fingers away from his wrist, so he pulled his body sharply from side to side, dragging Tarani along the floor.

She stayed with him, her body trailing his sword arm with a violent, jerking motion, until he swung the hilt of his sword at her head. She turned her face aside at the last minute, but the bronze hilt clipped her temple and she went down like a rag doll.

The guard looked around at Gharlas.

"Kill her," Gharlas said.

18

The fighting red haze of a sha'um's rage shot through me, burning away Gharlas's control.

In Dyskornis, Tarani had helped me fight that power. Given time now, I could have broken free on my own. But with a sword already descending toward Tarani's slender throat, I surrendered to Keeshah the control I denied Gharlas.

I seemed to be only a spectator, as my body lunged for the guard. I caught the man's throat in my hands and dragged him away from Tarani. He turned the edge of his sword against my back, but before it more than touched me, I threw him to the floor. I pinned his forearm with my knee and shifted my weight to that knee, slowly increasing the pressure on his arm.

His body bucked and heaved. His left hand beat against my arms, clawed out at my face. I leaned on neck and arm. The blows became so weak that I barely felt them.

I was delighted when his right hand opened to release the hilt of the sword.

I laughed out loud when I felt bones break under my knee.

I shook the throat I held, and the head wobbled back and forth.

Keeshah left me, and I was empty. I pulled my hands away from the dead neck. My fingers left blackening indentations in the man's flesh. The sight of them appalled me, but reminded me of the reason this man was dead.

I half-walked, half-crawled back to Tarani and put a shaking hand against the fair, unmarked throat. When I felt her pulse, mine started to move again.

I stood up and turned toward the big double entry doors. Gharlas was still there. His smile had become a grimace, and there was no mistaking the message of hatred that flowed from his glowing eyes.

"She's alive, Gharlas," I said, picking up the sword Tarani's would-be killer had used. "Your power won't work on me, and all your hired muscle is dead. In Dyskornis you said we would settle things 'another time'—*now*, Gharlas. Just you and I. We'll settle it now. I will leave this room with the Ra'ira."

I started down the middle of the long room, kicking aside the debris of broken furniture. Miraculously, the two tables which held the lamps were still intact.

Gharlas waited for me, his hand resting on the hilt of his sword. When I was a third of the way across the room, he cried: "*Stop!*"

There was a ring of confidence in his voice. Suspicion made me pause.

"You say 'you and I'," he sneered, "as if we were equals." He took a step closer, and the lamplight from the table nearest him sent wavering shadows from his supraorbital ridges leaping up across his brow. "But you're forgetting who I will be."

"'King of Gandalara'?" I mocked him. "You're a fool, Gharlas. You can't even hope to rule Eddarta, much less all the cities and towns scattered around the Walls. What are you planning to do, mind-control all the Lords?"

"Such crudeness is unnecessary," he answered. "Pylomel's influence rests with his fortune—when the Lords discover it is worthless, that *I* have the wealth he pretended to have, and that *I* have the loyalty of the Harthim guards, I will be acclaimed High Lord."

He might be right, at that, I thought. *Political rules in this city, though they make a show of being traditional, seem to be largely a matter of convenience.*

"What about Indomel? He won't let you take over without a struggle."

"I see you have learned a lot about Eddarta since you arrived," Gharlas said. "Until my plans are ready, I will allow Indomel to act as High Lord—under my control."

"All day, every day? Even with the Ra'ira, do you really believe you can do that?"

"All I need, at first, is subtle control at key moments, and the ability to know what the boy is thinking—those things the Ra'ira can give me easily. But if brute, total control is necessary? That, too, is within my power. For example . . ."

The door beside Gharlas opened, and Thymas walked in.

"You remember this young man, don't you?" Gharlas said. "Without Tarani to help him, he is completely mine. How delightfully ironic that you gave him Serkajon's sword for 'safekeeping.' I look forward to having that sword— after he kills you with it."

Thymas came toward me, the steel sword held lightly in front of him. I shifted my weight to face him. I didn't back away.

"When we decided to follow you, Gharlas," I said, keeping my eye on the slim, muscular boy approaching me slowly, "we all knew the odds, and agreed that the stakes were worth any risk. Thymas knows that I won't hesitate to kill him to get to you."

Thymas stopped, about ten feet away from me. His body reflected the struggle inside his mind. Muscles stood out on the sides of his neck, throwing into bright relief the ugly scar left by the vineh. A vein at his temple pulsed in a slow, heavy rhythm that seemed to symbolize the boy's determined resistance to Gharlas's power. His arms and hands trembled with the effort to break free of that terrible compulsion.

"He wants it that way, Gharlas," I said, still watching Thymas and feeling a fierce pride in the boy. He was fighting with everything he had, fighting so hard that I could *feel* the strain. "If the only way he can help me get to you is by dying, then Thymas will make it easy for me to kill him. He'll slow down at a crucial moment, leave openings in his defense."

I glanced at Gharlas, and was jolted by what I saw. His eyes widened, his breath started coming faster, and the smooth line of his jaw bunched out as he clenched his teeth. Thymas took another step forward—stiffly.

Come on, Thymas! I thought, excitement growing in me. *If there's one thing you are, it's stubborn. Don't let go! Don't give in!*

"You see?" I gloated. "All you've done is bought a little time, Gharlas. You picked on the wrong man. You can't use Thymas as a weapon again; *he won't let you.*

"You want ironic? You sent assassins to kill Dharak, and they attacked me by mistake—and both of us were the wrong targets. For you, *Thymas* is the most dangerous man of the Sharith."

I heard two sounds simultaneously, then. One was a moan from Gharlas, the other was a word whispered by Thymas: "Sharith."

"He's weakening, Thymas," I encouraged the boy. "You can break him! Keep trying!"

Thymas and I were together now. I fought Gharlas with words of encouragement, and the boy's entire body was quivering with the intense strain of what he was trying to do. We both knew that if he couldn't break free of Gharlas's control, one of us would have to kill the other.

"Sharith..." Thymas gasped, more loudly this time.

"Sharith... *kill their enemies!*" He jerked forward, as though he had been pressing against a physical barrier that had just given way.

Thymas gave a yell of triumph, and we whirled toward Gharlas. He had turned his back to us, and seemed to be dancing, stepping quickly from one tile to another in a rhythmic pattern.

Has he flipped out for good? I wondered. Then it dawned on me.

"The secret passageway!" I shouted, and started running. Thymas was right beside me, but we were already too late. Gharlas pressed on a section of the wall; it moved back to reveal the top steps of a narrow stairway leading downward to our right. One of the lamps stood on the table right beside him. He caught up the light and vanished down the stairway, leaving us in near-darkness. The wall section started moving back into place, unnervingly silently.

We reached the door an instant before it came flush with the rest of the wall. It pushed back on its bronze tracks easily enough, though it was heavy.

"Hold it while I get a lamp," I told Thymas. "If it closes, it'll lock, and we'll never figure out the sequence of tiles to push to open it again."

He leaned against the tall slab of wall, but demanded: "Is Tarani all right? Where is she?"

"There were five guards waiting for us," I said, as I got back with a lamp and an extra sword. "Tarani got knocked out in the fight, but I'm pretty sure she's all right. We'll brace this door open, so she'll know where we went."

We squeezed together on the few inches of landing inside the wall, and let the door begin to slide past us. I held the spare sword at waist level until the hilt was firmly caught. Then we started down the stairs, single file.

Like everything in Gandalara, Troman's Way was well constructed. Long, narrow slabs of marble lined the walls and supported similar ceiling slabs. The floor of the passageway looked like cobblestone, set directly into the earth to allow for both a dry walking surface and a means of draining off the moisture that seeped through the marble joinings.

The place stank abominably; the walls and rocks were covered with a growth like mildew that seemed to shrink away from our lamp as we passed by.

We tried to hurry, but we couldn't run across those slick rocks. The direction seemed right to take us under Lord Hall, but it was hopeless to try to estimate the distance we were covering. It seemed like hours before the passage ended in a narrow stairway, much like the first one, leading upward.

The door at the top was closed, but there wasn't any sort of lock that we could see. Cautiously, our swords ready, Thymas and I pressed our shoulders against it; it gave way easily.

We stepped sideways from behind the door, pushing aside a heavy tapestry. We were in the High Lord's treasure vault, which seemed to be L-shaped. We were facing straight down the long leg of the L, with the shorter branch leading off to our right.

Marble shelves stair-stepped up both long walls of the long wing, leaving a narrow walkway toward the end of the room, which was invisible past our circle of lamplight. A richly textured fabric was draped across the shelves, and against its dark background shone a dizzying array of gems, jewelry, and coins.

I glanced at the floor and noticed that it had tiles similar to that in Gharlas's house—just as I heard the soft whisper of the door as it moved back into place.

I whirled around and snatched at the tapestry, and discovered that we had come out through a section of a massive, wall-long woven scene. I fumbled around the shape of the receding door, but by the time I found the edge of the section, the door had closed and relocked.

"You can't get it open." It was Gharlas's voice, coming from the end of the shorter wing of the room. Our lamp cast enough light for us to see all the way to the far wall. Gharlas wasn't visible. I felt my skin begin to get restless.

"Throw down your swords, and I may let you live," the disembodied voice said.

Where the hell did he get all that confidence again? I wondered. *He was running scared when Thymas broke through; what could he have found here? . . .*

"Pretty clever, Gharlas," I said. "What better place to hide the Ra'ira than in Pylomel's own vault."

"You're remarkably quick, Rikardon, I must grant you that. Yes, I chose to face you without the Ra'ira for two reasons. First, it was an excellent test of how close one must be to the gem to utilize its special powers—closer, obviously, than from here to the pitiful quarters Pylomel assigned to me. Second, I was slightly concerned that the girl's mind-gift might also be able to work through the Ra'ira. Now that she is no longer involved, I have no further hesitation. *Do as I say: put down your swords!*"

"Show yourself, you cowardly bastard!" Thymas shouted. "Come out and face—*acchh . . .*"

His voice choked off, and he clutched at his throat with his free hand. I knew what he was feeling; my windpipe was closing more slowly, with a pressure that made me feel some pity for the big man Keeshah and I had strangled.

This was a stronger force than I had felt before. I could resist it more effectively than Thymas, but I wasn't immune to it. I would die of asphyxiation more slowly; that was all.

I never really believed we could lose, I realized, as I gasped for breath. *I felt so strong, with Thymas and Tarani on my side. I figured I might get killed, but not all three of us. But—damn it!—Gharlas is winning! There must be something more we can do, SOMETHING!*

With the onset of the attack, a light had appeared near the end of the short passage. Now Gharlas stepped out from around a hidden corner, carrying his freshly lit lamp in one hand. The Ra'ira rested on the palm of his other hand.

19

The lamplight penetrated the smooth surface of the gem, sparkled along the faint lines that marked its strange internal structure, then jumped out at us again. Gharlas's hand was bathed in blue light, his face lit from below with the pale edges of that reflecting glow. He walked toward us, insane, insufferable satisfaction on his face.

Keeshah! I called. *Can you help me again?*

I will try, he promised. I could sense that he had been running, and that he had reached the outskirts of the city. He was tired, fatigued by the frustration of not being with me, and on the brink of desperation because he could sense my doubt. We had broken Gharlas's power once this way, and I had yet to see Gharlas make the same mistake twice.

Not yet, I told Keeshah, and I deliberately slowed my breathing. Panic was the last thing I needed. *He needs to be closer. I'll tell you when.*

But Gharlas stopped when he was only halfway down the room. Stopped, smiled, and pushed harder with his mind. Thymas dropped Rika and fell to his knees; I knew he had only seconds more to live.

The door behind the tapestry pushed open with a slight, but audible sound. Gharlas's attention wavered for an instant.

NOW, KEESHAH! I signaled, and the sha'um's consciousness surged into my mind like a muscle flexing

134

against a binding. Gharlas reeled backward, and Thymas started taking deep breaths.

The man with the Ra'ira stared at us in astonishment. It didn't take telepathy to guess that he was suffering through the same revelation I had faced moments before. He knew he'd lost.

He threw his lamp to the floor; the glass chimney shattered, and the candle nearly went out.

Keeshah started to withdraw from me, but I held on for an instant. There were no words to the message we shared—only gratitude and joy. The exhilaration that comes only after a close brush with death, or after nearly losing a loved one. And I realized, belatedly, that in merging with me, Keeshah had endangered his own life. He would not have withdrawn until it was over, win or lose. It was conceivable that, so closely linked with me, the great cat would have died with me.

Together soon? Keeshah asked, when the link had faded.

Just as soon as possible, I promised, then returned my attention to Gharlas.

I was too slow. Thymas had been a single breath away from passing out, but he had reacted immediately when Gharlas let go. Gharlas, sprawled at Thymas's feet, was absolutely still. When I reached them, Thymas was using Gharlas's sleeve to clean the blood from Rika's blade. He was still gasping, trying to catch his breath.

Thymas bent over, then straightened and held the Ra'ira and the lamp base. He turned the gem over, examining it near the candle flame. Then he pushed it toward me. "Here, take it," he said gruffly. I hung the lamp I carried on a bronze hook, and held out my hand. Thymas let the blue stone drop into my palm, just as we heard Tarani's voice.

"Thymas?" it said, sounding muffled. "Is that you? Where are you?"

We looked back to see the tapestry bulging around the door. The far edge of it flapped, and Tarani appeared at its edge. She looked around cautiously, and her face lit up when she saw us. She put her lamp down and came running the length of the room.

"Thymas," she cried, and threw her arms around him. "I'm so glad to see you!"

He hugged her joyfully, lifting her off her feet to whirl her around. There wasn't much space, so I moved out of the way. A cold, dead weight was hanging in my chest. To take my mind off of it, I busied myself trying to identify a familiar, whispering sound.

"The door!" I shouted. "Don't let it lock again!" I dashed to the tapestry and for the second, frustrating time, failed to block the door.

"What's the matter?" Tarani asked.

"What's the matter?" I raged, whirling on her. "We can't get out of this fleabitten place, that's what's the matter!"

"Rikardon," she said, coming down the room toward me. The light behind her showed the lines of her body through the loose-fitting desert tunic and trousers. "Are you all right?"

"You're the one we need to worry about," I said, grabbing her arm to turn her around so that her disturbing outline didn't show. I held her chin up and examined the bruise on the left side of her face. She flinched away from my probing fingers, and seemed about to say something.

"There's another door here," Thymas called. "Gharlas was trying to get out." He dragged the long body back around the corner where Gharlas had first appeared, then came back. Tarani and I met him at the doorway. "There's another treasure room over there, just like the one we were in, and just as full."

"Zefra said this door will open into the Council Chamber," I said, running my hand along the surface of the door. It was wooden, and not quite smooth. "Unfortunately, I forgot to ask her for a floorplan of Lord Hall. We might come out smack in the middle of the Celebration Dance.

"Tarani," I said, without looking at her, "do you think you could manage a three-way illusion to cover us, until we get out of the Hall?"

"I will do what I have to do," she answered.

"Maybe this will help," I said, and put the Ra'ira in her hand. For a moment, she looked as though she wanted to drop it, but then she closed her fingers around the blue gem.

"Ready?" I asked. They nodded.

We leaned on the door.

It didn't budge.

We tried again, pushing harder, and this time it moved a fraction of an inch. Sideways.

Suddenly the small depressions in the surface of the door made sense. We each gripped and pulled to the right. It moved—slowly at first, then so quickly that it slid to the end of its bronze runners with a determined clang that sounded as loud as a gunshot.

We moved through the large opening, tensed for another fight, but all we found was the empty Council Chamber. We were on a raised area at one end of a room which seemed to be about as long as the treasure rooms, but more than twice as wide. The one chair on the dais faced a rectangular table that did a fair job of filling up the room.

There were seven other chairs. Six were identical to the one near us—carved from wood, their backs and armrests adorned with etched metal plates—but they rested on the floor, a level below what could only be the High Lord's chair. There were three of these on each side of the table. The seventh chair was little more than a stool at the far end of the room.

The door started sliding shut. It was bigger than the opening through which we had stepped. It was nearly six feet wide and as tall as the nine-foot ceiling. Made of layers of wood laminated together, it was four inches thick. And if that weren't enough, covering it on this side was a thin sheet of bronze, decorated with a lot of tiny geometric designs.

I don't know how the Eddartans rigged that one-way spring system. The door was so well balanced that one man could open it. Thymas and I both put our weight and muscle against it, trying to *keep* it open. But it was determined to close, and we had to snatch our hands away at the last second to keep our fingers whole.

"Now what?" Thymas asked.

"Same plan," I said. I pointed to the far side of the room. "Different door."

"Wait," Tarani said. "Zefra must be nearby. Let me call her in here, Rikardon. She can tell us what to expect and I—I can say good-bye. I promised her," she added, a little defensively.

Thymas said: "Let's get *out* of here."

"And I promised *you*," I reminded Tarani. "Do it. But keep it short." She nodded, then sank into one of the chairs and leaned back, holding the Ra'ira in her lap. She closed her eyes for a second, then said: "She's coming."

Using her power is getting easier for her, I thought. *That's another reason to get her out of here.*

I started pacing. Thymas started looking at the figures on the bronze face of the door, and Tarani just sat there, waiting.

I was at a loss to explain the sense of urgency I felt. A number of explanations occurred to me, all of them plausible, none of them precisely right.

Now that we had the Ra'ira, I was eager to get it away from Eddarta.

Knowing I was probably surrounded by the Eddartan "nobility" made me itchy.

Certainly, I was looking forward to hugging Keeshah.

Where are you now?￼* I asked him.

In the city. Smells. Can't find you.

We're up on the hill, but you wait there. We'll be down soon. Has anybody seen you?

In answer, he sent me a flash of what he was seeing: a crowd of people, carrying torches, following him at a respectful distance. I saw something else that made me glad—Ronar was with him.

Nobody bothers us, Keeshah said. I would have laughed at the understatement, but my nerves were too jumpy. I was half-afraid I'd get hysterical.

A soft click warned us that the entry door was opening.

Zefra slipped through, and let it swing shut behind her. "So Troman's Way *does* exist!" she said. "Gharlas?"

"Dead," I said.

"Good. You . . . recovered what you came for?"

Thymas gave a small start. "We found the gold, yes," I said, and out of the corner of my eye, I saw Thymas relax. Zefra noticed him. "May I present Thymas, of the Sharith? Thymas, this is the lady Zefra, Tarani's mother."

Thymas was prepared to greet her respectfully, but Zefra merely glanced at him, nodded coolly, and started to walk past him. But she stopped, abruptly, near his left arm, and swung on him in a fury.

"You *dare* to bring that vile thing before the Bronze?" she demanded, and reached out as if to snatch up Rika's gleaming blade where it hung free of Thymas's baldric. "It was a symbol of trust between King and Guard, until the Guard turned its blade against the Kingdom. What *insolence* to bring it here!"

Tarani grabbed her mother's shoulders and pulled Zefra away from Thymas, who had jumped back with his hand on Rika's hilt.

So much for not judging the Sharith, I thought.

"How dare *you* insult our friend?" Tarani demanded of Zefra, yanking her around. "You speak of the distant past, Mother. That sword has no meaning here except that it has saved our lives."

Confronted by her daughter's anger, Zefra blazed up. "No meaning, you say? The *distant* past? You are mistaken, Tarani. The past is here in this room. As the Bronze is the symbol of the Kingdom, so is that sword the symbol of its destruction!" Zefra had shaken loose from Tarani and climbed to the dais. She touched the massive piece of decorated metal, almost reverently.

"This is the Bronze. It was created here in Eddarta, at the command of one of the early Kings. It was installed in Kä, to be the final test for one who would be High Lord. Harthim brought the Bronze back to Eddarta, and mounted it as you see it here. No one, other than the Lords and High Lord candidates, has ever seen it before."

She turned around and fixed her gaze on Tarani. The peculiar intensity I had seen before had returned to her face, and I thought that even Tarani saw it now, and was a little frightened.

"I was wrong to attack your friend, Tarani. There is meaning in his presence here with you. It is a signal that you can command the loyalty that Harthim lost.

"A message lies hidden on the Bronze, daughter. The very mind-gifted can read the message, because the All-Mind knows what it says. The mindpower has weakened in us through the generations since Harthim, and most of the message has been lost. I have heard that only the first few words are still readable."

Zefra went to Tarani and put her hands on the girl's shoulders, turned her to face the huge, patterned door. "But you can read it, Tarani. I know it. Read the message of the Bronze," Zefra breathed to her daughter.

My skin crawled.

"There is nothing here but meaningless decoration," Thymas said.

"There *is* a message!" Zefra cried. "This is the old writing. The message was imprinted first, then other markings were added to make all the characters look like the master figure. Those who have the power, whose link with the All-Mind is strongest, can see the original inscription."

"We don't have time for this," I said.

Tarani's back stiffened. "I think this is little enough to grant in return for all the help Zefra has given us."

I controlled my impatience, and nodded assent. Thymas moved restlessly away from the wall Tarani was going to "read".

Now that Zefra had explained the markings, I found some knowledge of the "old writing" in Markasset's memory.

Gandalaran characters were made up of lines joined in precise angles or crossing one another. Modern writing employed brush and ink on paper, and considerations of speed and appearance had allowed the development of curves and longer lines in writing style. But the original characters were based on the "master figure" Zefra had mentioned: eight short, straight lines, radiating from a common center at precise forty-five-degree angles from one another. Every character was made up of *some* of those lines.

I looked at the Bronze, and all I could see was the master figure, repeated over and over again. All the tiny marks were imprinted to exactly the same depth, were exactly the right length—the vertical and horizontal markings slightly longer than the intermediate lines.

But Tarani looked at that wall full of nonsense and started to read out loud. At first she read slowly, hesitating over every word. Then she began to read with more confidence.

I stared at her in amazement, and I noticed that she had the Ra'ira, hidden inside her clenched hand. Whether that was helping her, or her own native power was doing the trick, I couldn't have said. Zefra watched her daughter with a look of rapture as she and Thymas and I listened to Tarani's voice speaking a message from the distant past.

20

I greet thee in the name of the new Kingdom.

From chaos have we created order.
From strife have we enabled peace.
From greed have we encouraged sharing.

Not I alone, but the Sharith have done this.
Not we alone, but the Ra'ira has done this.

THESE ARE THE WEAPONS
OF WHICH I GIVE THEE CHARGE
AND WARNING:

The Sharith are our visible strength—

Offer them respect; . . .
Be ever worthy of their loyalty.

The Ra'ira is our secret wisdom—

Seek out the discontented;
Give them answer, not penalty.

THIS IS THE TASK I GIVE THEE
AS FIRST DUTY:

As you read the scholar's meaning
Within the craftsman's skill,
So read within yourself
Your commitment

To guide
To lead
To learn
To protect

142

> *If you lack a high need*
> *To improve life for all men,*
> *Then turn aside now,*
> *For you would fail the Kingdom.*
>
> *I greet thee in the name of the new Kingdom,*
> *And I charge thee: care for it well.*
>
> > *I am Zanek,*
> > *King of Gandalara*

I was totally stunned. Not just by the fact that Tarani had read the thing. Not even by the nobility of its message. The signature was what got to me.

Zanek? Zanek had the Ra'ira when he created the Kingdom? But Thanasset said the stone had been sent to Kä when the corrupt Kings began to demand tribute, which was ages after Zanek's day. Maybe Thanasset, and the other Supervisors, prefer to think that the Ra'ira was used only during the bad times, so they can justify keeping it in Raithskar.

I don't know the answers. But I do know that there is no more relationship between Zanek and Pylomel than between me and a vineh. That foolish gem belongs in Raithskar, where Pylomel and his kind can't get to it.

Zefra had Tarani—who seemed a little dazed by what she had read—by her shoulders, and was shaking her lightly. "You see? Yours is the strongest mindpower in generations, Tarani. You are meant to be High Lord. It is why you came here."

Tarani pulled out of her stupor to push away her mother's arms. "So that we can rule your way, instead of Pylomel's? Mother, were you not listening? Zanek warned that the power of the Ra'ira could be used well or badly. He was a good man; I could sense that from the message. But there are few like him in the world today." Her voice trembled. "Volitar was one. I thought you might be another, but I see I was wrong. No matter what you say you want, Mother, you are not much different from Pylomel."

Zefra gasped, and hauled back her hand, and slapped Tarani. The girl accepted the blow, and faced her mother again.

143

"I offer you my thanks, Mother," she said. "For your protection of me all these years and, now, for giving me proof of the rightness of our duty. We *must* get the Ra'ira back to Raithskar, where it can be protected."

"*Tarani!*" I said sharply. Her intake of breath told me she realized her mistake, but the damage was already done.

"You *have* the Ra'ira?" Zefra whispered, and began to plead. "Think of it, child. You could be High Lord. The changes you could make. The good you could do. The things that Volitar believed in—you can make them real! If you have no other ambition, merely keeping Indomel from becoming High Lord would be a thing worth doing."

A new voice, high-pitched and full of sarcasm, sounded from behind us. "What a loving thing to say, Mother."

We whirled around to see a handsome boy, tall and dark-furred, close the entryway door. He walked through the room as if he owned it, and stopped a couple of paces away from the women. Thymas and I were both on the other side of the table, with our hands on our swords. But he made no move toward the jeweled dagger that complemented his rich clothing—a floor-length tunic of green covered by a heavier, sleeveless tunic in a deeper tone of green. He just looked Tarani up and down in an appraising, insulting way.

"I grant you that this lovely creature is talented," he said. "I felt the compulsion she sent to you. I didn't understand what it was, until I saw you sneaking into the Council Chamber—where you have no business being.

"I caught the door before it quite closed, and I heard almost everything, but I'll be glad if you'll confirm a few things. For instance, I gather that Gharlas is dead?"

"Yes," Zefra said.

"I should be grateful for that, I suppose. My father is many ways a fool, but never so seriously as when he permitted Gharlas to win the favor of the Guard. My first act, as High Lord, was to be the destruction of Gharlas— an unnecessary task, now."

He walked slowly beside the table, letting one long-fingered hand caress the back of one of the huge chairs.

"I heard another name that sounds vaguely familiar," he said. "Volitar?"

"He was my father," Tarani said. "A good man. Gharlas killed him."

I wondered what she thought of the self-possessed boy who faced her. She showed no affection or revulsion, merely wariness.

"Ah, I remember, now—the jeweler who disappeared before I was born, around the same time as my mother's infamous escapade. Or should I say 'our mother,' since it appears you are my half sister?"

"No," Zefra said, with a fierceness that made the boy retreat a step. "How often I have longed to say this to you, Indomel. Tarani is your *true* sister, your elder, the rightful candidate for High Lord."

"What are you saying?" Tarani demanded.

"*Pylomel* is your father," Zefra said. "The night he visited me, the night before I left Eddarta—he *compelled* me to lie with him, and how I hated him for it. I didn't have the power, then, to resist him completely, but I managed one small defiance—I hid it from him that I was fertile, and that I had conceived.

"But I told Volitar the truth, that I carried a child with a great gift—I could already sense it, Tarani. I feared to raise you in Lord City, for Pylomel would have taken you from me. Volitar understood. He took me away. He loved you like his own daughter."

"I *am* his daughter!" Tarani cried. "Everything I am, Volitar gave me. I refuse to accept that—that filthy old man as my father!"

Indomel laughed with genuine humor, but the sound of it was sour.

"An apt description, sister, and a wise choice. We who are in this room believe that you are my full and true sister, but should you claim that before the Lords, you would find it difficult to prove. All you have is the word of a woman who has been locked away, by choice, for many years, and who is generally spoken of as eccentric, if not actually insane." He smiled. "A reputation I have encouraged at every opportunity, dear Mother. You see—Tarani, is it?—our lack of affection for one another is entirely mutual."

Tarani's neutrality vanished. "You are a monster," she said.

"Yes," he said agreeably. "And I have power that not even our dear mother suspects."

Suddenly, there was pain. Not the concentrated hurting that Gharlas had inflicted, but a general, intense pain. It struck. Thymas, Tarani, and I flinched, gasping. It receded.

Indomel was smiling.

I really hate this, I thought. *Aren't we ever going to get out of this bizarre place?*

"I can use a less . . . exotic form of compulsion, as well. Your friends look formidable, Tarani, but could they defeat the entire Guard? No, I think not."

"She is your *sister*, Indomel!" Zefra cried.

"So you say, Mother, and so I must believe. Because of that, and because this is the eve of a great day for me, I am feeling generous. Tarani and her friends may leave here alive—on condition that they never return to Eddarta, and that they leave the Ra'ira with me."

"Do not take us for fools, Indomel," Tarani said. "We have not come this far to give up now."

"I am not often generous, sister, as you should have learned by now, if only from Zefra's teaching. Why don't you consult with your friends? I can't imagine two healthy young men sharing the company of such a delightful creature without becoming totally devoted to her. How do they feel about your being the first to die?"

Tarani jerked convulsively, then doubled over, moaning in pain, and Indomel sighed. "You may have a strong gift, Tarani, but it is limited by your kindness. I have no such restraint on mine." He waved his hand, as if in dismissal. "I have nothing to fear from you."

"Then let her go!" I shouted, running around the table

146

to put my arms around the girl. Thymas was right behind me.

"Stop hurting her," he growled, "or I will cut your hands off and feed them to you."

Indomel, self-assured as he had seemed until then, took a step backward before Thymas's ferocity. Then he straightened his shoulders and spoke with some bravado: "I will stop when I have the Ra'ira."

Tarani gasped: "No!"

I stared at Indomel, projecting my hatred. I hoped that, if his power could penetrate my "double-mindedness", the strong emotion would mask my plans.

"It isn't worth Tarani's life, Thymas," I said. I opened the pouch at my belt and pulled out the duplicate we had brought from Volitar's workshop, that Gharlas had wanted so desperately to possess.

Indomel's long, thin fingers took the glass piece from my hand. He turned it over once, looking at it carefully; then Tarani stood up, free of pain. She kept one hand clenched around the real Ra'ira; the other hand reached for mine and pressed it tightly.

"The Ra'ira," Indomel breathed, looking through the blue "stone" toward the light. He was trying to seem only politely interested, but his breathing had quickened. He was beginning to see the implications of what he *thought* he had.

"There have always been legends, of course, that this beautiful bauble had some power of its own. How I shall enjoy learning the truth of it.

"How did it come to be in Eddarta?" he asked.

"Gharlas stole it from Raithskar," I answered shortly. "You said you would let us go."

"Oh, yes, certainly. Go on. I'm sure my dear sister can provide you concealment as you move through the celebration. You may wish to pause a moment, and have a dance or two. What are you waiting for? Go on." His eyes never left the blue stone as he waved us past him.

We moved down the room toward the entry door. Tarani

147

turned back to her mother. "Zefra?" she said uncertainly. "Please . . ."

"I will stay," Zefra said. "I—regret striking you, Tarani. I heard Volitar's words in your voice, and they shamed me. But I cannot change now, daughter. Go carefully . . . and be safe."

Tarani waved her hand slightly, then pulled herself around to face the chamber door. Music and laughter greeted us as we opened it. A short corridor lay before us. Beyond the open entryway we could see the food-serving area of the party, a chaotic collection of tables and servants.

Without bodies blocking sight of our actions from the Council Chamber I took the Ra'ira from Tarani's unresisting hand, and put it in my pouch. We sheathed our swords and joined hands.

"Ready?" Tarani asked.

Thymas and I nodded, and the three of us stepped out into the Celebration Dance.

21

The door moved behind us, and we heard the muffled sounds of a struggle. We jumped back into the concealment of the hallway and whirled around.

Indomel was pressing back against the stone wall, fury and amazement plain in his face. His mouth opened and closed, but made no sound.

Zefra stood near him, not touching him. She was glowing with triumph. "He planned to betray you to the Guard," she said, then smiled grimly. "But I have power that not even my dear son suspects. I can control him—for a time. With your help, Tarani, *we* could control him—always. Perhaps he is right, and you could not be acclaimed High Lord. But we could use *Indomel* himself, Tarani, to bring about the changes we know are right. I ask you again: stay."

Tarani hesitated.

I thought, again, how much the two women resembled one another. Height, facial structure, bearing—it was uncanny. Could I blame Tarani for feeling the call of a common heritage that was so plainly visible to all of us?

What will I do if she wants to stay? I wondered. *It's her choice. Please, Tarani . . .*

She said, softly and sadly: "No."

Zefra sighed, and I started to breathe again.

"Then go quickly, daughter," Zefra said, and opened her hands to show us what she held. "I will keep the Ra'ira." She watched us warily, prepared for some argument.

"Keep it, then," Tarani said. "But don't rely upon it, Mother—remember that the Kingdom fell, without it."

"Thymas. Rikardon."

The commanding tone of her voice hid the grief I knew Tarani must be feeling. Deceiving Zefra was *necessary*. Using her power to help us get away was *necessary*. Leaving her was *necessary*.

But the only thing that made it *possible* for Tarani was the glimpse she had been granted of her mother's desire for actual power. There was no stronger argument for securing the true Ra'ira than the way Zefra, who knew the corruptive influence of power better than most, coveted that harmless piece of blue glass.

So we turned away and started once more across the dance floor. I felt Tarani's hand trembling, and I knew she was close to collapse. Possibly for that reason, she had assumed the familiar semblance of Rassa, and given me the look of Yoman. Thymas she had not changed physically, but she had given him, as well as us, clothing appropriate to the occasion.

We moved around the tables slowly, only pretending to be surveying the selection of refreshments. Ahead of us was the door which led to the main avenue of the city—and to the entry gate. To our left and right, the ballroom flowed around the Council Chamber that was the core of Lord Hall. People milled and danced, laughed and talked. And one particularly large group had planted itself directly in front of the door we were heading for.

Is it possible to die of impatience? I wondered, as Tarani shifted our path into an arc which would swing around the knot of people. *I'm going to jump right out of my skin, any minute now.*

The group of people was in a constant state of change, with individuals leaving, joining, or working their way through. Just as our arc began to swing back toward the doorway—it was barely twenty paces away, now—someone broke away and stepped right in front of us.

It was Pylomel.

"Doubtless you have forgotten our appointment for later

this evening," he said softly. "Lovely Rassa. I look forward to it now, more than ever." He reached up to stroke the golden hair he thought he saw—and Tarani wasn't up to coping with a tactile illusion. As his hand touched her hair, the entire illusion vanished.

I reached for my sword, but Pylomel didn't raise the alarm. His mouth sagged open, his eyes grew large, and he sank to his knees, holding onto Tarani for support. She pushed him away, shuddering.

People looked around, just as Pylomel fell over. When they saw the hilt of Thymas's dagger protruding from the High Lord's chest, just under his rib cage, somebody screamed.

We drew our swords and headed for the door, three deadly points on our triangle. Nobody near us was going to be a problem—there was a lot of yelling, and a general and uniform scramble to get out of the way. I was surprised at the contempt I felt as I thought: *They're so used to having everything done for them—including their fighting*.

Trouble is, I thought in the next second, *they've got people to do it*.

There were four guards in the doorway, waiting for us to get clear of the crowd.

Thymas and I attacked, leaving Tarani to keep the mob at bay. Apparently Gharlas had appropriated the best fighters for his own plans, because these four were rookies. In seconds, they were all dead or badly damaged, and the three of us ran out into the avenue.

Lamps had been placed on platforms along the main avenue. We had a clear view to the city entrance. The river, with a line of rafts tied up by its bank, was barely visible, though we could hear its rushing murmur clearly above the clamor coming from Lord Hall.

We ran like hell along that lighted pathway, then skidded to a halt, not a hundred yards from the gate. Where I had expected two guards, maybe four, there were twenty. And they had heard the ruckus. They were ready for us.

Tarani groaned, and Thymas swore: "By the Nine! Is

there no escape from this fleabitten place? Not even the sha'um could fight these odds!"

Damn Eddarta and its blasted Celebration Dance, I thought. And its blasted hired muscle. These guys know it'll be their skins if we get away. Thymas is right, we're trapped. Unless—

This was a Gandalaran situation, and suddenly I was thinking like Ricardo, who saw *two* gateways into—and out of—the city. "Come on," I said, and dragged Tarani toward the line of tied rafts. Thymas followed. The guards set up a yell and started running down the avenue.

I let go of Tarani's hand and jumped from the bank onto one of the rafts. It wobbled in the water; I dropped to my knees to steady it for Tarani's arrival.

But Tarani and Thymas were standing on the bank, staring at me in confusion.

"What are you doing?" Thymas demanded. "There aren't any vleks, and anyway they would be too slow—what are you *doing*?"

"Shut up and get out here!" I ordered.

Tarani dropped to all fours and crawled out to me with teeth-gritting slowness. I put my arms around her and could almost feel her terror through her skin.

She knows what's going on, I thought. But she came anyway.

Thymas was still on the bank, and he had figured it out, too. "That's crazy!" he said. "You'll kill us all!"

Two lines held the raft against the shore. I slashed one, and the raft swung out toward the current, Tarani and I balancing precariously on our knees. "You want *them* to kill you?" I asked. He looked over his shoulder at the oncoming guards, fifteen yards and closing. Then he turned back and took a deep breath.

"No, don't jump!" I warned, too late. He landed on the tied corner of the raft. "Grab him!" I told Tarani, and sliced through the last line.

By some miracle, Thymas didn't send us all into the river. "On your stomachs," I yelled. "Spread your weight on the surface of the raft." Daggers and swords flew

152

overhead as the raft drifted away from shore. A couple of the guards, either braver or more desperate, ventured out into the water after us, but retreated when it got too deep to walk.

I didn't have any trouble getting Thymas and Tarani to hang on to the ropes that lashed the reeds into logs, and tied the logs together. They were terrified, and probably seasick, as the rudderless raft spun slowly toward the arch that marked the edge of Lord City.

The guards were running along the bank, arguing about what to do. Some of them were laughing at us; others were just plainly amazed. There seemed to be no question at all in their minds that we were totally, thoroughly crazy.

Things floated in Gandalara. Pontoon bridges. Rafts steadied by vlek power. *People* drank water, bathed in it, used it to irrigate crops. They did *not* float on it. It simply wasn't part of the Gandalaran lifestyle.

No wonder Tarani and Thymas were scared to death. I felt some of their fear, myself—but Ricardo's logic put a hammerlock on Markasset's traditionalism.

"Listen," I warned the others, "when we hit the rapids, we're going to get wet. *Don't let go!* Even if the raft breaks up, pieces of it will float."

The raft was through the archway, moving more or less straight and faster, now, toward the brink of the cataract. Tarani looked up, whimpered, and pressed her face back into the reeds. Thymas looked up, too, and watched grimly as the blackness of the empty Gandalaran sky seemed to rush toward us. A roar of falling water drifted up from the hidden slope of the hill.

"*HANG ON!*" I screamed, as the raft tipped sickeningly forward.

The raft plunged down the hillside, crashing against rocks, dipping and bucking like a thing alive and trying its best to get rid of us. It didn't matter that it was too dark to see; all our senses were concentrated on breathing, when we had the opportunity, and clinging to that bundle of reeds.

The raft took one deep dive, and when it bobbed to the

surface, it took us a few seconds to realize that we were level again. I looked up to see lights and the straight lines of the edges of buildings ahead of us.

I lifted myself cautiously to my hands and knees, to make sure. We were at the inner edge of Eddarta. "Tarani, Thymas," I urged, "take a look. We made it."

Just then, the raft hit a hidden crosscurrent and spun wildly. My knees slipped, and I wound up half in, half out of the water, my weight canting the surface of the raft at a crazy angle.

"Rikardon!" Tarani cried, and started to come after me.

"Stay there!" I ordered.

We had drifted into the city itself, now, and there was a crowd of people, carrying torches, on the riverbank. I wasn't sure how they knew we were here, or what they thought of us, but the immediate problem didn't relate to them at all. As far as I could see, we were spinning slowly, and not making much speed downstream.

All right, smart guy, I thought to myself. *How the hell are you going to get this thing back to ground? Didn't think about that, did you?*

My hands were stiff and chafed, and I was beginning to swear at the weight of the gold around my waist—but when I thought of it, the solution occurred to me.

"Thymas!" I called. "When I move, you move along the opposite edge, to keep us balanced. Tarani, you stay put. Understand?"

They both nodded, and Thymas released each hand in turn, working out the stiffness in preparation of moving around.

I was hanging off the raft from its side, so that water was striking abreast of the reed log. I started pulling myself along the log by its lashings; Thymas crept along the far edge in the other direction. It was tricky, turning the corner, but worth it—with my body weighing down the log ends, the current channeled itself along the ridges, and the spinning motion stopped. When I had worked my way into the center of that edge, we started moving downriver with some speed.

Only now there was a new problem. I couldn't get back up on the raft. The lashings which held the logs together were too close to the end of the raft to give me any leverage, and the next set which could provide a handhold was too far away to reach. All I could do was hang on.

Rikardon? The thought struck my mind, and I realized that it had been repeated before—I had been too busy surviving to recognize it. The small mystery of how the crowd of people had spotted us in the dark was solved, too—they were following the sha'um.

Keeshah! I called. *Follow the raft down the river.*

"Tarani, untie the middle lashing of the raft. Don't cut it unless you have to."

She started working at it with one hand and got nowhere. Thymas readjusted his position, and their two hands, together, loosened one knot. It was slow going, and I was beginning to wonder if my arms would hold out—but at last they had a good length of the sturdy, woven rope free.

Thymas—who, of course, was aware of the sha'um—had already seen what I had in mind. He pulled Tarani down to his end of the raft, tipping me out of the water for a moment, then moved nearly to the middle and stood up cautiously. He tied one end of the rope to another lashing, then threw the other end toward the bank. It fell far short, and he dragged the rope back, talking to himself.

"I'll try to guide us closer to shore," I shouted at him. "Tell me when you think we're close enough for the rope to reach." I strained my aching arms and pretended I really was a rudder, holding my body rigid with the legs pulled up at an angle. I could feel the difference in the water pressure against my body.

I'll be damned! It's working! I thought, and suddenly I had new energy.

Even that second wind was gone, by the time Thymas called to say it was time. I took a deep breath, let go with one hand, and dragged along underwater, fumbling with the fastening on my homemade belt. Finally it was free, and I spent my last bit of energy swinging the long, heavy thing up to the deck of the raft.

Thymas grabbed it, tied it to the rope, and threw it at the shore, nearly all in one motion. None too soon, either, because without that belt I made a rotten rudder. We were already moving toward the center of current again.

I craned to see the shore, and was surprised that we had left most of the city behind. The crowd of torches was still there, the huge shapes of the sha'um clearly silhouetted. There was a roar of noise from the nearly invisible people.

I had told Keeshah what we were doing, and I assumed Thymas had told Ronar. I saw the belt arc through the torchlight, and heard it slap into the ground and slither toward the river as we moved away from the bank. Keeshah went after it, pawing at it like a kitten chasing a string—and then he had it in his teeth.

He dug his claws into the muddy shore and yanked—and Thymas pitched head over heels into the water. He surfaced near the raft; I grabbed him and held him up until he was able to get a grip on the lashings.

The sha'um hauled us in leapfrog fashion, one pulling until the other had a jaw grip on the rope closer to the bank, then circling around while the other pulled.

When we scrambled to shore, we didn't take time to say hello. Thymas caught up the weighted belt, cut it free of the rope, then leaped on Ronar's back. I mounted Keeshah, and Tarani swung on behind me. The half-circle of torches opened where we aimed.

Wet, Keeshah complained, then carried us out into the night beyond Eddarta.

22

For more than two hours we ran through the pale moonlight. We passed through grainfields that looked like thick black carpet. We pounded through pastures, scattering grayish shapes—terrified vlek and glith.

I pressed my face into Keeshah's fur and didn't think of anything at all, for a while, except the exhilaration of riding again. There was an open, flowing contact between my mind and Keeshah's that was like a mental hug. There was little deception possible in our relationship; we each knew how glad the other was that we were together again.

Gradually my awareness expanded to include the others who were with us. Thymas and Ronar were a single, moving shadow off to my left, and Tarani was a warm pressure against my back. A hooting call from above told me that Lonna was nearby. For a breathless moment, I felt the bonds which tied me to each of them.

They were different—less intense, less intimate—than the special touching Keeshah and I could share. But I felt them.

It was an amorphous feeling, and very brief, like a glimpse into the heart of a brilliant diamond when, just for a second or two, you can *almost* perceive the structure of the faceting. You can *almost* understand—not the crisp angles and cool planes of the stone, but the *art* of the gemcutter who chose them and executed them.

It went beyond simply a sense of shared destiny—the team spirit of which I had spoken in Dyskornis.

It went beyond gratitude that each of them had saved my life.

It went beyond pride that, together, we had accomplished what we had set out to do—that we were carrying the Ra'ira back to Raithskar.

Team spirit, gratitude, pride. None of them quite identified what I felt, yet they were all part of it. I reached for the truth with all my intuition, but the moment passed too quickly. I felt my failure to understand as a piercing, cold ache, an inconsolable sense of loss.

I sought comfort in the steady rhythm of Keeshah's movement. After awhile, the stinging sadness eased, and I slept.

I woke when Keeshah's rhythm changed. *What?* I muttered sleepily to the sha'um.

Other one stops, Keeshah told me.

I came fully awake in a hurry. Tarani's weight stirred slightly as I moved, and I thought: *Could she be asleep, riding second? She must be utterly exhausted. And she hasn't recently recovered from Thymas's injuries . . .*

I suffered a twinge of pure panic as I opened my eyes. We seemed to be in a narrow corridor with walls so tall that I couldn't see over them from my present eye-level, which was Keeshah's shoulder height. I thought that we had gotten turned around, and were back in Eddarta.

"Thymas!" I called, sitting up. Tarani, startled into wakefulness, put her arms around my chest to steady herself.

"What's wrong?" she asked. Her cheek pressed my shoulder for a moment, then lifted. "Where are we?"

I felt foolish as the disorientation faded. Sitting up had brought my line of vision above the obstructions beside us, and I could see that the "walls" of the corridor were lattice frames covered with leafy growth. We were on a farm, in a Gandalaran version of a berry patch. The frames were about ten feet long, and stood in rows about six feet apart.

Thymas's head popped up, two rows away and some thirty feet behind us. "Here," he said. "What's the matter?"

"Nothing," I said. "I was asleep—"

"You woke suddenly. When you didn't see me, you assumed that I had fallen behind, *once more*, isn't that right?"

He said it with a bristling finality that dared me to contradict him. I could see him well enough in the pale moonlight to read sullenness in the shape of his mouth, resentment in the set of his shoulders.

I tried to count to ten. I got all the way to two.

"Sure, that's right," I agreed. "You're our weak link, Thymas. You and Ronar. Of course I have to look out for you all the time." I could find no trace in myself of the gentle kinship I had sensed earlier. "I was so afraid you'd just quit on us that I gave you Serkajon's sword to bring to Eddarta. You might fail *us*, I reasoned, but you'd never shirk your fleabitten Sharith duty!"

"Rikardon!" Tarani shouted, pulling at my shoulders. "You will regret what you have said. Be silent now."

Thymas looked grim. He was walking Ronar along the row of frames, coming opposite Keeshah.

"I've coddled this fool with my silence long enough," I said. "Now I'll say what he's wanted to hear—that he's been a stone around our necks ever since we left Thagorn. He lied to his father when he promised to obey me. His *actions* have sometimes been obedient, but his *thoughts* never have. Twice, Gharlas has used him to try to kill me. I can't help but think there was a predisposition in that direction before Gharlas took a hand."

Thymas was facing me, now, across the top of the barrier. He was deadly calm. "You're right about that last, Rikardon. Let's get out of this field, and settle it. I'll even give you back Serkajon's ever-precious sword."

"I don't want to kill you, Thymas—for Dharak's sake. And I don't need Rika to loosen your tusks."

Keeshah and Ronar leaped away, running down the parallel rows to the end of the field. Tarani was beating on my shoulders, shouting something I refused to hear.

When we reached an open meadow, I slid off Keeshah's back, knocking away Tarani's clutching hands. Thymas

159

landed on the ground at the same time, berries showering out from the cupped hem of his tunic.

I threw myself at him.

He ducked my swinging fist, and tripped me. I went down and rolled; his stomping foot hit the grassy stuff instead of my throat. He was on me again as I got to my feet. I let my balance shift backward, flipping him over my head as we fell. I jumped for him, landing on the ground as he rolled out from under just in time. He got to his feet and swung a kick at my ribs that connected with breath-stopping power.

I caught the leg, pulled him off balance, crawled up his body, felt the satisfaction of my fist slamming into his jaw.

Suddenly, there were three of us on the ground, wrestling. Tarani had thrust herself between us and was pushing us apart, taking some of our blows and delivering a few of her own in the process.

"Stop it!" she was yelling. "For Zanek's sake, will you two fleasons *stop it!*"

It was as though I were waking from a dream. The meadow was gray and silver in the moonlight. I could sense the vine-frames looming behind me. I could *see* Keeshah and Ronar, facing each other across us, their thickened tails and standing neckfur clearly revealed in silhouette against the grayish sky.

I sat on the ground, looking at Tarani, and remembered the sting of her hand across my face. Thymas, too, seemed stunned by the girl's fury.

"Fools!" she was raging. "Both of you—*fools!* Will you do to yourselves what Gharlas could not?" She stood up, making a sound of contempt. "If I thought Keeshah would carry me alone, I would take the Ra'ira and go. Indomel would be delighted, I'm sure, to find you fighting each other."

"Indomel?" Thymas echoed. "But Zefra was controlling him."

"Believing that her power was increased by the Ra'ira," I said. "That extra strength won't last long. Then they *will* send out pursuit."

"If I were in his place, I'd let us go quietly," Thymas said. "He thinks *he* has the Ra'ira—if we were caught, we could tell others."

"He is obligated to avenge the death of his father," I said. "He will make a show, at least, of pursuing us. And if he finds us, you can bet we won't have much chance to do any talking."

Thymas stared at me for so long that I wondered if his mind had slipped away. Then Tarani said: "Of course—you did not know that the man you killed was Pylomel."

"The High Lord?" Thymas said, still trying to understand. He surged to his feet, went to Tarani and touched her arms. "Your *father*, Tarani . . . I didn't know, I swear by the first King."

The girl jerked herself away from him. "*Volitar* was my true father," she snapped. "The sha'um can outrun any pursuit Indomel may send," she said. "Shall we go on?"

"Not together," Thymas said. He pulled Rika out of his baldric, and turned to face me. The blade shone softly in the moonglow.

What little refreshment I had gained from my nap on Keeshah's back had been drained away by our brief, explosive struggle. Where I wasn't actually cut or bruised, I ached with weariness. The desperate strength that had kept me going through the fight with Gharlas and the riotous trip down the Tashal was utterly used up. I knew, and the boy knew, and Tarani knew, that if Thymas wanted to kill me, he could.

He grabbed the long steel blade, and offered me the hilt of Serkajon's sword.

"I knew why you gave me this at Stomestad," he said angrily. "Am I a cub, to be tricked and teased into doing what I promised? Take it back, and free me from this 'team'. You have the Ra'ira. Our purpose is finished."

Numbly, I reached out and accepted the sword. The hilt felt cool and *right* in my hand, and I realized how much I had missed having Rika with me. I pulled myself to my feet, drew the sword I carried, and offered it hilt-first to the boy.

"I had to surrender your sword to a Lord City guard, Thymas," I said. "Take this one, for now. When I return to Raithskar, and our purpose is *really* finished, I'll replace it with the best sword I can find. Something worthy of the next Lieutenant."

Thymas lifted the bronze blade, and slipped it through his baldric.

"I never meant to let you think you weren't trusted or important," I said. "We'd have failed without you. I saw what it cost you to throw off Gharlas's control."

And to overcome your conditioning about water, I thought. *It took guts to jump out to that raft. Only I can't say that without explaining why I wasn't horrified by the very concept of floating on a river.*

"I can't say it's always been a pleasure, Thymas, but riding with you and Ronar has been an honor. I owe you a life-debt many times over. If you ever need someone to guard you . . ."

Hesitantly, I held out my hand.

Thymas had seen me use the handshake, before, as a parting or greeting gesture. He gripped my hand with a warmth that surprised me. It must have surprised him, too; he seemed embarrassed as he spoke.

"We share that life-debt, Rikardon," he said. "I respect your sword, and I've learned to respect your leadership. I can't yet call you a friend, as Dharak does. But I do call you Captain."

It was the last thing I expected to hear from Thymas. I was too stunned to speak. I walked over to Ronar, and offered my left hand, palm up. He dipped his head, and the stiff/softness of whiskers and fur grazed my palm. I reached up to stroke the fur along his cheek. That was a liberty usually permitted only to a sha'um's rider, and I was pleased that Ronar allowed it.

I discovered that my voice was working again. "It has been good, riding with you," I told the sha'um, then turned back to Thymas.

He and Tarani were locked in a close embrace, kissing. I

stared in shock, too tired to be embarrassed, in too much physical pain to feel the inner hurting. Much.

When they pulled apart, I said: "Go with him if you want to, Tarani."

"Why would you think she wants to come with me?" Thymas asked, his chin hooked over Tarani's arm, which still rested on his shoulder.

I made an indefinite gesture to indicate their present physical arrangement. "Why wouldn't I?"

"Because she *loves* you," he said. "She told me so in Stomestad."

Before I could hold it back, I stammered: "But—but I *saw* you, the night before we left..."

Tarani dropped her arms and stepped around Thymas. "You *saw* us?" she demanded.

"Accidentally," I hurried to say. "I was walking by the room—"

"Is that why you—?" She stopped herself abruptly, with a glance at Thymas. I couldn't tell in the dim light, but I thought she was blushing.

"No," I said. "I told you, Thymas had nothing to do with that."

"With what?" Thymas asked, plainly bewildered. When neither one of us answered, he shrugged. "Well, Captain, what you *saw* in Stomestad was a good-bye to what Tarani and I once shared. I had fewer regrets than I expected; Tarani had changed, and you and she seemed to belong together. We promised friendship, but our love isn't forgotten. Do you begrudge me a farewell kiss?"

"It may not be farewell," Tarani said, looking at me. "Rikardon suggested I go with you. Perhaps he wants it that way."

A sound startled us all. Thymas was laughing. It was the first time I had heard his laugh; it was a full, hearty noise that cracked through the tension in the air. He walked to Ronar and mounted, still laughing. As the sha'um stood up, he said: "Maybe if I leave you two alone, you can start talking to each other. And that's one conversation I'm not sorry to miss." He took a deep breath. "I think I understand you better, now, Rikardon. You're still the strangest man I've ever met—and you and Tarani are well matched. You'll both be welcome in Thagorn at any time."

"Thank you, Thymas," I said, and pulled my attention away from Tarani. "Give Dharak my best regards."

"I will," he promised. He waved a hand to me, and then to Tarani.

Even after Ronar's running figure had disappeared, I stood still, staring off into the distance, not the least surprised that I already missed the boy. Tarani's hand on my shoulder drew me back to the present.

I turned and held her closely, gently.

Go soon? Keeshah asked.

"Keeshah is restless," I said, still holding Tarani. "We do have some talking to do... can it wait?"

I felt her head moving against my shoulder as she nodded. Keeshah crouched, and we mounted, Tarani riding second, as usual. There was special meaning to the weight of her body against my back.

Take us home to Raithskar, I told Keeshah, and let myself really relax.

It's a little-known fact of life, I thought sleepily, *that, now and then, the odds* have *to turn in your favor.*

END PROCEEDINGS:
INPUT SESSION THREE

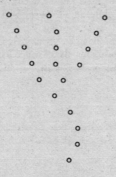

—*I shall withdraw our minds from the All-Mind . . . and mine from yours . . . Is the Record now complete?*

—*This portion of it is complete, yes.*

—*Will you wish to Record again?*

—*Someday the full accounting must be made to the All-Mind. But, as you promised, the Recording process is fatiguing. I must rest before I can begin the next portion. May I call upon you again, Recorder?*

—*At any time. I am at your service.*

ABOUT THE AUTHORS

RANDALL GARRETT, a veteran science fiction and fantasy writer, and VICKI ANN HEYDRON, a newcomer to the field, met in 1975 in the California home of their mutual agent, Tracy E. Blackstone. Within a year, they had decided to begin working together and, in December 1978, they were married.

Currently, they are living in Austin, Texas, where they are working on the Gandalara novels, of which *The Steel of Raithskar* is the first, *The Glass of Dyskornis* second and *The Bronze of Eddarta* third.

OUT OF THIS WORLD!

That's the only way to describe Bantam's great series of science fiction classics. These space-age thrillers are filled with terror, fancy and adventure and written by America's most renowned writers of science fiction. Welcome to outer space and have a good trip!

☐	22855	**CINNABAR** by Edward Bryant	$2.50
☐	20499	**LENSMEN FROM RIGEL** by D. Kyle	$2.50
☐	22588	**THE SUICIDE PLAGUE** by E. Naha	$2.75
☐	01355	**THE DINOSAURS** by B. Preiss & Wm. Stout (A Large Format Book)	$12.95
☐	13031	**THE ROBOT WHO LOOKED LIKE ME** by Robert Sheckley	$2.50
☐	20310	**THE EINSTEIN INTERSECTION** by S. Delaney	$2.50
☐	22938	**THE WINDHOVER TAPES: FLEXING THE WARP** by Warren Norwood	$2.75
☐	23394	**THE WINDHOVER TAPES: AN IMAGE OF VOICES** by W. Norwood	$2.75
☐	20752	**HONEYMOON IN HELL** by F. Brown	$2.25
☐	22968	**THE MARTIAN CHRONICLES** by Ray Bradbury	$2.75
☐	14144	**MOCKINGBIRD** by Walter Tevis	$2.95
☐	14274	**THE MAN WHO FELL TO EARTH** by Walter Tevis	$2.25
☐	01266	**LITTLE, BIG** (A Large Format Book) by John Crowley	$8.95
☐	22948	**STAR TREK: THE NEW VOYAGES 2** by Culbreath & Marshak	$2.50
☐	20990	**A CANTICLE FOR LEIBOWITZ** by Walter Miller, Jr.	$2.95
☐	20761	**SUNDIVER** by David Brin	$2.50
☐	22998	**THE FARTHEST SHORE** by Ursula LeGuin	$2.75
☐	22563	**A WIZARD OF EARTHSEA** by Ursula LeGuin	$2.95
☐	20594	**VALIS** by Philip K. Dick	$2.50

Buy them at your local bookstore or use this handy coupon for ordering:

Bantam Books, Inc., Dept. SF, 414 East Golf Road, Des Plaines, Ill. 60016

Please send me the books I have checked above. I am enclosing $_____ (please add $1.25 to cover postage and handling). Send check or money order —no cash or C.O.D.'s please.

Mr/Mrs/Miss_____

Address_____

City_____State/Zip_____

SF—4/83

Please allow four to six weeks for delivery. This offer expires 10/83.